ALISTAIR TE ARIKI CAMPBELL was born in the Cook Islands in 1925. His father, John Archibald Campbell, was a New Zealand trader, and his mother, Teu, was the elder daughter of Bosini of Tongareva (Penrhyn Island).

After the death of his parents, in 1933 Campbell came to New Zealand, where he was educated at Otago Boys' High School and Victoria University of Wellington. He then trained as a teacher, before joining the Department of Education, where he edited the School Journal for 17 years, subsequently working for the New Zealand Council for Educational Research, as senior editor, until 1987.

Campbell has published ten collections of poetry including *Mine Eyes Dazzle* (1950), *Sanctuary of Spirits* (1963), *Wild Honey* (1964), *Blue Rain* (1967), *Kapiti: Selected Poems* (1972), *Collected Poems* (1981), which won the 1982 New Zealand Book Award for Poetry, *Soul Traps* (1985), and *Stone Rain: The Polynesian Strain* (1992). He has also written numerous radio plays, a stage play, *When the Bough Breaks* (1974), and an autobiographical work, *Island to Island*(1984). His first novel, *The Frigate Bird*, was published in the Pacific Writers Series in 1989 and its sequel, *Sidewinder*, in 1991. Both were regional finalists for the Commonwealth Writers Prize.

Since leaving the NZCER, Campbell has been writing full-time. He was Victoria University Writer's Fellow for 1992. He lives in Pukerua Bay, 25 kilometres north of Wellington, with his wife, Meg, who is also a poet.

GW00402015

Tia

ALISTAIR CAMPBELL

PACIFIC WRITERS SERIES

First published 1993 by Reed Books,
a division of Reed Publishing (NZ) Ltd,
39 Rawene Road, Birkenhead, Auckland 10.
Associated companies, branches and representatives
throughout the world.

ISBN 0 7900 0282 5

Published with the assistance of the Literature
Programme of the Queen Elizabeth II Arts Council.

Printed in New Zealand

CHAPTER ONE

THINGS ARE NOT going well. I have never expected or hankered after a free ride through life. The gods owe me nothing, and I have never sought their favours. If I have burnt any candles at all, it hasn't been to any of them, but rather to my muse, and then usually at both ends – if you take my point. I want only to live quietly with my darling Tia and my family – but what writer ever had a moment's peace when ridden by his daimon? Add to that the knavery of the archfiend Sidewinder, and you'll have some idea of what I'm going through. In a word – it's hell!

You are confused, gentle reader? Well, you can be sure you're not as confused as I. You may recall that I boarded the calibration flight in Penrhyn, together with other passengers, including a distant cousin from Te Tautua – the one with a large gold tooth in the upper jaw, which he liked to display in a perpetual grin. Not that he's a genial fellow – far from it. He has an ungovernable temper. Big and powerful, he'll knock down anyone who he considers has slighted him. He had to be restrained by three of our bigger villagers from knocking senseless a simple young man Puku, a hunchback, who had called him *porangi*, mad. The safest policy I soon learned when dealing with him was to twinkle back at his twinkling tooth. But I wander off the subject.

Why was I confused? You may recall that an air hostess attended to me when the heavy scent of *tipani ei* in the cabin gave me a punishing headache – she brought me an aspirin. I can still feel the softness of her breast as she leaned against me to let a stretcher go past, carrying a patient swathed from top to toe in bandages. The only part that wasn't covered was a large glutinous eye that winked wickedly at me for the brief moment that the stretcher stopped. I knew at once who it was – Sidewinder! And the stretcher bearers? Who else but the imps Belial and Beelzebub.

Anyway, to come to the point, calibration flights as a rule never carry passengers. And they certainly don't have an air hostess on board. I think that's where Sidewinder made his mistake. And the reason? He rarely thought through any of his devilries. He was too impatient, too cocksure, and as a consequence he often fell into the hole he had dug for his victims. It's not surprising he remained – or so I gathered – in the second, or even the third order of demons. He had forgotten – if he'd ever known – that calibration flights are for checking equipment at airports and airstrips to ensure it's working properly. They do carry the odd passenger at the pilot's discretion, and on this occasion Gold Tooth and I had been given the nod. What about the crocks who had come aboard when we did? you may wonder. Illusions, cheap tricks designed to delude me into thinking this was a normal flight.

If the air hostess wasn't *bona fide*, who or what was she? While we were thundering over the Pacific I racked my brains, and in time the answer popped up like a slice of bread in an electric toaster. Of course – she was one of the passengers who shared my cabin on my first return visit to Penrhyn! She was a pearl buyer who lied about being married to a Penrhyn Islander. 'He not married to a Penrhyn man,' growled another of my cabin mates, when told about her claim. 'He married to an Aussie fella.' I remember seeing her at Omoka, huddled with a villager presumably buying pearls – but might she not have been trading in souls?

To say I was jittery would be an understatement. My hands were sweating, and if I had opened my mouth I'm pretty sure she would have heard my teeth chattering. I turned round slowly in my seat, cricking my neck in order to see her. She was a few seats behind me, talking to Gold Tooth. Her eyes narrowed when she caught my gaze, and out fell her tongue, black and stubby as a parrot's. I don't know why I found that as horrible as I did. Perhaps I could imagine human souls, my own included, being cracked like so many seeds, caught between the thrusting tongue and the incisors.

Yes, indeed – it was Living Doll all right! Squeaky clean, as I remembered her, every hair in place, dangerous, she stared back at me with all the insouciance of a cobra – to change the image. Gold Tooth also looked at me, then at her, then back at me. Someone had to give way, but I was determined it wasn't going to be me. My very life depended on it. Gold Tooth began to look uneasy. You may wonder if he was also part of the conspiracy. No. He was a violent man, but not essentially evil.

Have you ever tried to stare anyone out? Avoid it, if you haven't. I have known grown men to lose their temper and come to blows rather than acknowledge defeat. My eyes were beginning to smart when I suspected that she, too, was beginning to feel the pinch, for she resorted to cheap tricks in order to win. She would poke out her ugly tongue a full metre, making me duck, and wave it about; press the tip of her nose until I could see right up her nostrils; open her eyes to their fullest extent, then narrow them and bare her pointed teeth in an expression of the utmost ferocity, growling all the while. I survived all these and more, and in fact I couldn't stop myself from smiling at such childish tricks, and this I could see was upsetting her. Gold Tooth meanwhile was trying to signal me with his mouth and eyes, and he was no longer advertising his gold tooth, but trying to warn me. 'Go easy' was how I read it, but I was in no mood to listen. I was certain I could win.

Then my hopes went down the gurgler. I saw out of the corner of my eye an erect figure in pink, mincing down the aisle towards me. Again Gold Tooth flashed a warning, and I hurriedly turned round to face the fiend – for that's who it was – and I lost the contest. The effect on Living Doll was quite extraordinary. She didn't destroy me as I feared she might, but became friendly and solicitous, asking me if my head still ached, and would I like another aspirin. She even stretched out a talon to feel my forehead, and I began to relax, until a cry from Gold Tooth brought me to my senses.

'Don't let her touch you,' he blurted out, his naturally deep voice shrill with alarm.

'Bless my soul,' came that voice that had become as familiar as my own. 'What's the matter with the fellow?'

I braced myself and turned to face the demon, and was disconcerted to find him smiling fondly at me. And would you believe it, he was in drag!

'How do you like my outfit?'

'My G-G-God – a drag queen!' I stammered. It was clear he would stop at nothing to possess my soul.

'Will I do?' he simpered, pirouetting on the tips of his toes and almost losing his balance.

A barely suppressed giggle from Gold Tooth was instantly silenced by Living Doll snapping, 'I shouldn't laugh.'

'Well,' said the fiend, flirtatiously, patting the back of his hair, as elegantly as his lizard claw would allow. Typical, isn't it? It was a detail he had overlooked.

'Ahem,' coughed Living Doll, raising her talons and wiggling them to catch his attention, and then pretending to be scratching her cheek when she caught my eye.

Sidewinder got the message, and the claw was immediately replaced by an exquisite feminine hand, soft and supple, which he waved towards me, releasing a cloud of scent which had me choking.

Living Doll looked at me, then raised her eyes to the ceiling, as if to say, 'There's no helping some people!' It was rank disloyalty, which could come in handy one day. It could even save my life. I stowed the information away for future use.

All this time the fiend was drifting about, humming dreamily, giving what I supposed he thought was a moving impression of a romantic young girl in love. And that crawler, Gold Tooth, I heard murmuring with his frog's voice, 'How beautiful – oh, exquisite!'

Toady! I shot him a contemptuous look. Not that that did any good. His gold tooth gleaming, he was gazing at Sidewinder with the besotted eyes of a schoolboy in love. It was a revolting sight. There was no doubt he was bewitched, and this was confirmed when Living Doll looked at me and winked. Well – who knows? – she could be useful one of these days.

While Sidewinder is busy admiring himself pirouetting as much as the limited space in the aisle permits, let me describe him.

He has on a bright pink wig, rather like Harpo Marx's woolly top, but finer like candyfloss. His dancing shoes are also pink, as are his full-length stockings, bodice, and frilly ballerina skirt. What amuses me is the size of his shoes. They are like paddles, and it is truly amazing that he doesn't trip over them more often.

'Well,' he said, at last, slumping exhausted into the seat beside me. 'Beauty is so difficult, so very difficult – as you must know being a poet.'

Gold Tooth chose this moment to applaud loudly, shouting, 'Bravo, bravo,' until a withering look from Living Doll silenced him once more.

'I can't do without my admirers,' Sidewinder confided, gaining his breath. 'You must know about that. It's the drug that finally finished off poor old Oscar. Art is a hard mistress.'

I must say Sidewinder stank. I didn't like him being close to me one bit. He had splashed scent on himself, but through the scent came another smell which I can only describe as fetid. He stank of the marshes, an overpowering, clinging smell, which took me back to *Beowulf* which I studied as a student. Grendel must have smelt like that.

Sidewinder was maundering on. 'I know you admired my dancing. An artist can always tell when he's getting across to his audience. And you,' he murmured, placing a claw on my wrist. 'You are everything I like in an admirer.' I shot a glance at Gold Tooth to see how he was taking this flattery, but I got no reaction at all. He was staring blankly in front of him. Was he dead? Where was Living Doll? She had disappeared. That gave me quite a turn. What were they cooking up?

It then occurred to me that the ballet outfit, the crazy dancing, the inane talking, all had a sinister purpose – to lull me into a false sense of security, to catch me off balance, and then –

I became aware of the fiend following my thoughts. He shook his head and smiled sadly. 'You've got it all wrong. You must learn to trust your friends, dear boy.' The hypocrite then took out a large black handkerchief from somewhere on his person, wiped his eyes, and blew his nose noisily into it, and then – God damn the old phoney – gave me a sad tremulous little smile. Then he reached out and tried to pat my knee, but I would have nothing of it, and pulled my knee away. 'Dear boy,' he again murmured.

'I'm not your dear boy!' I shouted. 'Nor your dear anything else.'

My shout had the effect of bringing Living Doll running, but Sidewinder waved her away, impatiently. When she just stood there by the toilet door, he gave another, angrier wave, and she disappeared. I looked around for Gold Tooth, but he had also disappeared. This is probably the place to mention that she'd had him in the toilet, and had been trying to force his head down the bowl, and would have succeeded, too, if my shout hadn't distracted her. 'I bloody near drowned,' he told me later, tears in his eyes. It was obvious the experience had left him almost a mental wreck. Where was the bully boy now? I wondered.

'I'm still waiting,' murmured the fiend. 'I asked you how you liked my outfit.'

'Well,' I said, deciding to play along, 'it's certainly better than the winding sheet you were wearing when you came aboard.' Then a thought occurred to me. 'By the way, what became of the stretcher-bearers?'

'Never you mind,' growled the fiend.

'I rather liked them, and I have a sneaking feeling they rather liked me. They reminded me of Laurel and Hardy.'

At this the fiend guffawed, and the noise was so powerful it shook the aircraft. I looked out the window half-expecting the wings to fall off. 'Haw, haw, haw,' he bellowed, and my skin crawled, because I knew with a dreadful certainty that this was how the fiend laughed when he saw the Archangel Michael driving our first parents from the Garden of Eden. 'Haw, haw, haw,' came the echo from the rear of the plane where Living Doll stood, with Gold Tooth's head under her arm. 'My God,' I thought, 'she's beheaded him!'

Again the fiend applied the black cloth to his streaming eyes, gasped for breath, and then cried, 'My dear boy – you'll be the death of me.' Then he looked sharply at me and said, 'So, you got the connection all right – Harpo's woolly poll and all that? Only connect – you catch my drift? Good boy – you'll do me.'

Thirty thousand feet above the glittering Pacific feathered with wispy waves – and here I am cooped up with a dangerous lunatic. No way out – no possibility of escape!

'I'm talkin' to you, fella.'

He's talking with his Yankee voice – so I had better look out.

'Yes, I do think your frilly skirt is pretty,' I prattled, 'and I do love your smart red shoes. But where are the food stains?'

'What have food stains got to do with it?' Watch it, watch it, I told myself.

'Well,' I mumbled, 'when I first met you in the mental home–'

'Ah,' he murmured, 'the mental home – our friendship goes back a long way. In fact,' he went on, his voice dropping to a whisper, 'it goes back a long way further than that.' At the time I hadn't the foggiest idea what he was driving at, but I was soon to find out, at the cost of a great deal of pain.

'Go on,' he prodded.

'It's nothing really – but if you insist.'

'I do insist.'

'Well, your clothes were always splattered with food.'

'And you find that amusing?' Icicles formed in the air.

'Well – yes.' My throat constricted and I was barely able to squeeze out the next few words. 'But I may be mistaken.' I didn't like the look in his eyes so I hurried on. 'I've always thought it the badge of a mental patient – an honourable one.'

'Let me get this straight, bozo.' The Americanism again! 'Are you saying I was a mental patient?'

'Well, weren't you?' I stuttered. 'You were there when I was.'

'Precisely,' he snapped. 'I was there *only* when you were there. My master had a contract out on you, and I was chosen to carry it out. But enough of this shillyshallying. The game is up.' He put two fingers in his mouth and gave a loud piercing whistle, an unholy sound that caused every nerve in my body to pop. He paused, then whistled again, and this time from very far away I heard a clap of thunder.

Living Doll rushed into the cabin, shouting, 'What are you doing? You are calling up a storm.'

At that very moment, a gust of wind caught the aircraft side on, causing it to shudder and dip, before straightening up again.

'I must have given the wrong whistle,' stammered the fiend, as lightning flashed to our rear, followed by another roll of thunder.

'You fool,' screamed Living Doll, 'we almost had him. Another five minutes and we would have won.'

I had always been aware of a cowardly streak in Sidewinder, and to my ineffable delight it was now beginning to show. As the storm caught up with us, and with lightning flashing and sizzling along the wings, he stood in the aisle, licking his lips nervously, while his forked tongue tumbled out of his mouth. He was quite literally panic-stricken. His knees were knocking together and his pink candyfloss hair stood upright, emitting blue sparks.

Normally, I would have been terrified, because the full force of the storm was on us, but because it was the lesser of the two evils – the other being the loss of my immortal soul – I was jubilant, and jumped up and down, shouting like a schoolboy.

'You aren't thinking of leaving us, are you?' I jeered, as the aircraft dropped into a hole a hundred feet deep, and I laughed aloud. I tell you, I was nearly mad with joy.

'It's no laughing matter,' quavered the fiend. 'I would have thought you would have been as disappointed as I to leave our business unfinished.'

'Never,' I hooted. 'Go on – jump. Jump, you bastard, jump!' I looked around for Living Doll, and saw her hanging on grimly to her armrests, and glaring at Sidewinder.

There was an almighty crash and the aircraft shuddered and plunged like a boat going over a waterfall.

'Don't forget to take your two imps with you,' I shouted above the roar of the storm, and grabbed the back of a seat to keep my footing.

'They left long ago,' he screamed back. 'They must have known something.'

There was a sudden explosion and the two fiends disappeared, leaving the smell of sulphur in the air. And strange to say, no sooner had they fled the aircraft than the storm died away. It was uncanny. It was as if a hole had appeared in the sky through which the storm and its apparatus of thunder and lightning had been withdrawn, making an eerie whistling noise.

I saw Gold Tooth stumble out of the toilet, holding his dripping head in his hands. 'I drink too much. I went to the toilet for a piss and passed out. When I wake up, my head it was in the loo.' He was a sorry sight.

'What that fella whistle for?' he asked, wiping his face with his sleeve.

'What fella?' According to the rules, he shouldn't have heard him.

'You play games – I hit you. Only kidding. The fella that whistled.'

'Oh, that fella! The hounds of hell would be my guess.'

'The hounds of hell!' Gold Tooth thought it was a great joke, and chuckled as he buckled himself into his seat, and I followed suit.

I looked at my watch and was astonished to find that we were only an hour out of Penrhyn. So much had happened, it seemed much longer than that. An hour till we touched down at Rarotonga! I needed all that time to compose my shattered nerves, and sort out a number of disturbing details while still fresh in my mind. I could hear Gold Tooth snoring. I could expect no help from him.

I kept thinking about Belial and Beelzebub. When did they leave the aircraft? I felt I had to know. You may recall that back in Penrhyn these two demons had fallen out with Sidewinder over their improper use of the coffin which was intended for me. They had gone fishing in it! He had torn strips off them, humiliating them so much they had turned on him, and shoved him instead of me into the coffin. Ironical, isn't it? He saved my bacon – or rather the three of them had in their different ways.

Then I had another, more disturbing thought. What if the struggle had been a put-up job, carefully staged to allay my suspicions, and throw me off my guard, thereby making me vulnerable to more dirty tricks. I agonised over this, but reached no reassuring conclusion.

And who was Living Doll anyway? She was clearly a demon, but had she shared my cabin on that fated voyage to Penrhyn Island? Or had that been a real person, a pearl buyer, as she had claimed? And had Sidewinder merely borrowed her likeness for some dark purpose beyond anything I could imagine?

There was another, larger question. I remember reading about a student who was strolling peaceably down a Wellington street with friends when he was suddenly attacked and killed. A deeply disturbed mental patient had picked him out from the others as the one to die. It was random and motiveless.

As he lay dying of a deep knife wound, he looked up in anguish and asked bitterly of the world, 'Why me – why me?'

That describes my feelings exactly. The resolve to solve this riddle is partly what keeps me going.

We arrived at Rarotonga Airport in perfect weather, and as soon as I was in the terminal I looked for a telephone to ring Tia. She hates flying, and when we said goodbye on the airstrip I could tell from the tremor in her voice that she was terrified that the worst would happen. The plane would crash into the sea and she would never see me again.

'Oh, my darling,' she breathed, 'thank God you are all right. I was so afraid. Can you hear me? There's so much static.'

'I can hear you. I'm fine.' It did occur to me that Sidewinder might have been behind the interference, but I dismissed it as unlikely in the circumstances. The chicken had again flown the coop. He probably had a lot of explaining to do to his master.

'Did you have a good flight?' Tia's wavering voice seemed to come from very far away.

'It was bumpy at first, but fine towards the end.' I couldn't tell her about Sidewinder's latest escapade, because she is deaf to any mention of him. She simply blocks her ears – metaphorically speaking, of course – and just doesn't hear. It's a form of self-protection, I'm sure.

'Tieki misses you.'

'Really? I've only been away a few hours.' I was absurdly chuffed all the same.

'I thought you'd like to know.'

I could hear children's voices in the background, and a child laughing. 'Is that Tieki I can hear? I'd like to talk to him.'

'No – he's gone fishing with Uncle Vaka.'

'Well, give him my love, won't you – and, of course, the twins.' I'll have more to say about Tieki later, but I may as well mention here that on the tragic death of her aunt, who poured kerosene over herself and set herself alight, Tia had adopted two of her children – the twins. Uncle Vaka was their father.

'Have you rung the doctor yet?' came her voice through the heavy static. She had to repeat the question.

'No – not yet. I'll check in at the motel, and then get on the blower.' We exchanged a few endearments, then hung up.

I shared a taxi to the motel with a couple of Kiwis, a tall scrawny older man, and a hulking youth, who was obviously his son. They did nothing but squabble and snarl at each other.

'Oh, shut up, yer great galoot,' the father shouted at last. 'I was a mug to bring you on this trip.'

'A mug's right,' mumbled the son, ducking his head.

'Wassat you say?' bawled the other, raising his fist.

Oh, Lord, I thought, they're going to have a scrap!

'I didn' wanna come on this bloody trip, did I?' He snorted contemptuously at the raised fist. 'Put it away, Dad – ya might hurt yaself. Yer pathetic, ya know!'

I could see the taxi-driver glowering at them through the rear-vision mirror, but fortunately the men ran out of steam, and fell silent.

There was something familiar about the taxi-driver. You could tell from his movements he was an impatient, energetic character. Then the penny dropped. He was another of the passengers that had shared my cabin along with Living Doll. I had called him Muscles because he was a powerful man, with an explosive temper. I could see he recognised me also.

'You all right now?' he asked. 'You sick man on the boat to Mangarongaro.' This is the ancient name for Penrhyn Island. 'You better now?'

'Yes, thanks.'

I remember his telling me he ran a small store on the island, so I couldn't help wondering what he was doing here, driving a taxi. I was curious to find out, but I didn't know how to ask him, without giving offence. Fortunately he volunteered the information.

'My wife, she run off with an Aussie pearl-buyer bastard, so I say to hell with Penrhyn. I go to Raro to get a job, and this I done. The money it not good, but OK.'

'You sold the shop?'

He laughed bitterly. 'The shop no good. Lost money all the time. Lost my money, lost my woman. No good the Aussie man.' He spat out the window. 'You know that woman in the cabin with us?'

'I do.' I didn't mention that Living Doll was my name for her. It wouldn't have made much sense to him.

'Her husband he stole my woman. If I catch him I hit his head in.' And he thumped the wheel with his great fist, nearly causing the car to veer off the road.

Living Doll, I thought, and now Muscles! Fat Boy was the

remaining passenger who shared the cabin. When was I going to run into him? I had the frightening feeling that my past was beginning to catch up on me.

My old friend Miss Black, the manager, was in the office when I was filling in the register. She congratulated me on my marriage to Tia. 'I hope you'll be happy. She's a fine girl. Our hula troupe has never been the same without her.' She ruffled through some papers in a basket, and then asked casually, 'What brings you back to Raro? I had a feeling you were wedded to your island.'

It was a tricky question, and I didn't know how to answer it without going into intimate details. There were other ears beside hers that seemed to be waiting for an answer. The cleaning girl who had looked after my room during my previous visits was pretending to be interested in the notice board. And one or two guests were hanging about. So I said, simply, that I had a medical problem I needed advice on.

'I believe I did hear something on the Island grapevine.' Was she concealing a smile when she turned her head? 'Well,' she said, her head still averted, 'I hope it's nothing to worry about.'

'Amen to that,' I murmured, and was about to go on when she said, 'By the way, did that strange fellow catch up with you?'

'Strange fellow,' I quavered, putting down my bag, which the cleaning girl pounced on and spirited away.

'Didn't he fall down a mountain, or something?' She turned and confided in the scrawny Kiwi impatiently waiting to sign in. 'Covered in bandages, he was. A proper sight.'

She looked at me, slyly, her pupils greatly enlarged by her thick lenses. I had always found her a formidable personality. And the motel staff, men included, went in fear of her. I have seen the cleaning girls scatter like sparrows before a hawk, when she went on the rampage.

'Surely you remember him.'

I couldn't understand why she always had a dig at me whenever I stayed here. I remember my sister telling me that her dad and ours had quarrelled bitterly, but I can't remember what over. Could that be the source of her animosity? But how absurd. That was years ago. But, then, feuds and quarrels die hard in the Islands.

As to her question – yes, I remembered him only too well. It was Sidewinder she was referring to – obviously. Back in New Zealand, in the Southern Alps, I had dared him to jump from a hanging valley to prove he could be trusted. He had prevaricated, but I had forced him into a corner – in a manner of speaking, of course – and he had no choice but to jump, and it seemed he had broken nearly every bone in his body.

But did that put him off the hunt? Not at all. Like some sort of Frankenstein monster, swathed in bandages, he caught my flight to Rarotonga, pursued me to this motel, and then secretly boarded the ship to Penrhyn on which, in a last desperate effort to possess my soul – even if it meant cheating – he turned himself into a monstrous waterspout, and would have swept me to my death if I hadn't appealed to my grandfather. He heard my cry and came to my rescue, cutting down the fiend with the Archangel Michael's sword.

'No,' I said, deciding not to give her the satisfaction of knowing she had got through my defences. 'I can't say I do remember him.'

'Well,' she said, grinning broadly, 'it doesn't matter now. It's past history.' She thought she had won, and could afford to be generous.

She handed me the key. 'I've put you in your old room.'

CHAPTER TWO

I FOUND MY bag by my bed in my old room, but there was no sign of the cleaning girl who had put it there. But the room itself was just as it was when I occupied it two years ago, including the crab-like stain above the kitchenette sink. Although it was disfiguring, I didn't complain about it to Miss Black, because I'm a cancerian, and at the time I looked on it as a kind of talisman to ward off evil or misfortune. Was it for the same reason that I was protective of spiders which also have eight legs and a similar cancerian shape? Eight is, of course, a lucky number in the Penrhyn Island (Tongarevan) cosmology, the universe itself possessing eight skins or layers. Tia used to shake her head whenever she saw me lifting a spider out of harm's way, but then, like many women, she has a dread of spiders, amounting to a phobia.

'*Kia orana*' came a familiar voice, sweet and clear. It was the small cleaning girl who had made off with my bag. Her face looked freshly scrubbed and she wore a blue floral *pareu*. Her blue-black hair rippled down her back almost to her bottom. She exuded an almost succulent nubility.

'Oh, I'm sorry – did I wake you? I can come back.'

'No – I'm just lying down. Come in – do.'

'Miss Black, she sent me to see if you got everything you need.'

'I think so, but you could check the fridge.'

She made her way rather heavily across the room, and I could tell she was pregnant. She caught my glance and smiled shyly. 'I'm going to have a baby.'

'I'm pleased for you. Do I know your husband?'

'Oh, we're not married. We wait until we save the money for a house. Too many people in my parents' house, so me and my boyfriend live at his place in the meantime.'

She checked the contents of the fridge and said, 'It's OK – it's all here. Miss Black she says you ring if you want anything more.'

'Thank you – I'll do that.'

As she was about to go, she said, shyly, 'I hear you and Tia got married. She a lovely girl. You very lucky.'

'Thank you. I count my blessings.'

'Pardon?'

'It's just an expression which means I'm specially fortunate.'

'You have children already?'

She was as guileless as I remembered her, and I couldn't take exception to her prying. 'No. Sad to say we don't have children of our own. Tia, as you may know, has a son from her first marriage, and we adopted twins, both girls.'

'Tia can't have any more children?'

'The problem is mine,' I told her. 'I'm going to find out if anything can be done.' I didn't want to embarrass her with details, but, reader, I can tell you. The trouble started when I had a prostate operation, which effectively blocked the passage of the sperm, making it impossible for me to impregnate Tia through normal ejaculation. I am hoping that medical science is sufficiently advanced to help me.

'Is there anything else?' I asked. The cleaning girl was hovering about the door, as if reluctant to go.

'Yes,' she said, and hesitated. 'A man and woman were at the desk, asking for you. The man looked so funny in a teeny skirt!'

There it goes again – a bombshell! I have noticed that devils often choose the innocent as messengers of doom. 'Asking for me?' I mumbled, trying to keep my voice steady. 'I wonder who they could be.' I had the unpleasant feeling that the command of the situation had passed from me to her, and that in her innocence she was enjoying it. And a twitch in the corner of her mouth made me wonder if she were as innocent as I'd deemed her to be. 'These p-people,' I stammered, 'what did they look like?'

'The man was tall and skinny. He had pink hair standing up on

20

his head – you know, like he got a fright. He wore a little skirt, like, like – '

'A ballerina.'

'That's right.' Then she gave a little shiver. 'I laugh at him – he look so funny. But he look at me and I don't laugh any more.'

'And the woman – she was a woman, wasn't she, and not a man dressed as a woman?' I don't know why I bothered to ask.

The girl was now subdued. 'Oh, the woman! She – how shall I say? She too perfect like a waxwork. Oh, she so beautiful like your Tia, but not nice like her. She scare me, too.'

The living dead, I said to myself, and I think she must have read my mind, because she gave a little shudder.

'Did anyone tell them I was here?'

'Don't know. Not my business.'

'Good for you,' I said, giving her a grateful look. 'Look, if they turn up again, tell them nothing – mum's the word.'

'Mum's the word!' That expression cheered her up. She looked at me and laughed. 'I like that – mum's the word. My mum talks all the time. My papa he can't say nothing. She won't let him. So mum's the word, isn't that so?' She left the room, shaking her head and smiling.

Feeling exhausted, I looked at my watch, and was surprised to find I had left Penrhyn Island only five hours ago. It seemed much longer than that. I should have rung the Scottish doctor long before this, but I have kept putting it off. I don't know why. He was an irritable old bugger, I knew that from previous encounters with him, both in person and on the radio telephone. But in his gruff way he had given me good advice, and I had felt easier in my mind from having spoken to him.

Why did I hesitate now? Possibly because so much depended on my mission. Back home in Penrhyn, Tia would be anxiously awaiting my next telephone call, and I wanted to be able give her good news, but I had no idea what the doctor would tell me. It could be all bad. So I had hesitated. I almost regretted leaving Penrhyn, and possibly exposing Tia to further pain and heartache.

It had come as a bitter disappointment to her that I couldn't give her a baby, but she had come to accept it, and had begged me not to go. And here I was opening old wounds.

There was nothing for it – I had to ring the doctor. I found the number in the directory, took a deep breath, and dialled it.

'Hello, this is Dr Ruby's surgery. Can I help you?' A bright professional voice.

'Yes – I'd like to make an appointment with Dr Ruby.'

'I'm sorry, but he's in Australia. Can I help? I'm a doctor, too.'

'Well . . . '

'Can I ask who's speaking?'

I told her my name.

'You're a writer, aren't you – and didn't you ring from Pen-rhyn some time ago? My husband found it a most puzzling call and the static was particularly bad.'

'That was Sidewinder's doing,' I said, but I could have bitten my tongue off. The fiend must be pretty close, for me to lose control like that. How he must be grinning in his stupid ballerina outfit!

'I could fit you in later this afternoon.'

'When is Dr Ruby likely to be back?' Perhaps I am sexist, but I didn't want to discuss my problem with a woman, not even if she were a qualified physician, as this one claimed to be. And her annoyance at being slighted showed in her voice which became curt and chilly.

'I'm afraid I can't help you there. He's at a medical conference, and he may stay to the end, or he may not.'

There were other doctors in the directory, but I didn't know if any of them were competent to advise me, so I decided to fly to New Zealand. But first I must ring Tia and discuss my decision with her. I had mentioned this possibility to her, and she wasn't at all happy about it, and it was unlikely she would feel differently now.

Should I ring now, or wait till evening? I was pretty sure that Sidewinder and his moll – he won't like that, nor will she! Start again! I was certain the demon was lurking about, and would relish another opportunity to interfere with the sound waves. That bump

22

in the ceiling just then was a rather crude attempt at intimidation. I felt like shouting, 'You don't frighten me, you old drag queen, you!' but it would be too draining, and God knows I have little enough energy as it is.

I know what I'll do. I'll find out where he is – with the cleaning girl's help – and have it out with him. I just won't play his stupid cat-and-mouse game, and when he realises that, he might become bored and tool off, and leave me alone. And then again he might not. Always this doubt – anguish to me, but meat and drink to the demon!

And I must say I'm disappointed in the cleaning girl. That story about seeing the two demons enquiring about me at the desk – somebody put her up to it. It was too pat. If she had seen them, she would have been a mental wreck. No, I believe that Miss Black was behind it. I remember now why she has it in for me – my father beat hers for the job of resident agent on Atiu. Old man Black – what a trial he was to my sister, with his bony knees! How she hated it when he held her there, while something hard and unpleasant reached up at her.

I'll ring Tia this evening. It might be difficult to get hold of her today. A *tere* party from New Zealand is expected in Penrhyn tomorrow, and she may be at the church hall, helping with the decorations. There was a large group of people at the airport terminal this morning, half-smothered with *ei*. I recognised some of them as Penrhyn Islanders from Mangere and Porirua. I have to admit I'm glad I won't be there during the visit. Mere, Tia's mum, would have insisted I attend the interminable prayer meetings and church services, and I would have consented for Tia's sake and to avoid the confrontation that has become a regular feature of Mere's and my relationship. It would have been different, if I'd been able to give Tia a baby, or several babies – the more the merrier. Mere would have been able to hold her head high among her friends, most of whom have numerous grandchildren. Tia is her only child, and as Tia had produced a child before I came on the scene the fault must be mine.

I decided to call it a day, and repair to the beach bar for a couple of stubbies. But, first, I must check to make sure the coast is clear. Sidewinder could be lurking about. I part the curtain just enough for me to peer out. The sun shivers in waves on the paved courtyard between the two wings of the motel. Did the curtain twitch in the window opposite, and was that an eye that gleamed before the curtain closed again? A large pawpaw tree with its clusters of breasts partly obscures my vision, so my imagination could be playing me tricks. Anyway, here it goes.

I trot towards the kidney-shaped swimming pool, full of noisy bathers, splashing each other and laughing. A tall fair girl in a bikini, whose accent gives her away as an Aussie – 'Come on een – eet's terreefic!' – dives just as I pass her. I wait to see if her skimpy bra can withstand the impact. It can. I hurry past, taking care to drop my eyes before the feminine wares displayed so fetchingly on the grassy verges of the pool. And so to the circular beach bar with its picturesque thatched roof. Cooled day and night by the gentle trade wind, it's a popular watering hole.

'How you doin', boss?' The barman was a young man, with a badly scarred face. I recognised him as Tere, who had accosted me once in the restaurant bar a few years ago. He was very drunk and aggressive. He was an Atiuan shark fighter, he told me, and he pointed proudly to the scar, as if it were a badge of honour. He had then gone on to boast of his university degrees. If one were to believe him – and I wasn't so inclined – there was hardly a subject in the calendar he hadn't mastered.

'Don't I know you?' He glowered at me.

I took a long pull of ice-cold lager. 'That's better – it hit the spot.' I refilled my glass and said, 'Yeah, you should. We had a run-in a few years ago. But it came to nothing.'

'Ah, the writer.'

'Yep.'

'I seen you walk around with little bits of paper. What you write on the paper?'

I felt like telling him it was none of his business, but it was less trouble to be civil. 'I'm writing a novel.'

'Ah,' he said, 'you write for Mills and Boon – is that so? My woman she read Mills and Boon all the time. She a great reader. You must meet her – you get on together very well.'

'And I also write poetry.'

'Ah, I know – like that fella who write the daffodil poem.'

'Wordsworth.' I pushed my money across the bar, and said, 'Same again.'

'That's the fella – Worthwords.'

'No – Wordsworth.'

'What the difference – Worthwords, Wordsworth – he the same fella.'

So much for his self-proclaimed scholarship, I thought, as he slid another stubby towards me. Then he leaned across the bar, looked round him, and murmured, 'You need to watch out for a coupla women who come looking for you. They say it was a writing fella they wanted to talk to. You a writing fella, you say, so you must be the fella they want.'

'QED.'

'You all right?'

'Yes.' Which was a lie, because my heart had turned over. 'Looking for me, eh?' I said, steadying my glass. 'A couple of women, you say?'

'Yeah – a coupla women.' He began to laugh. 'One she had pink hair, and a tiny skirt like dancers wear – and, yeah, pink shoes, big as canoes. He could walk on water in them canoes.' Seeing the look on my face, he explained, 'He dresses like a woman, but he a man.'

'And the other woman?'

'Oh, she a woman, all right – no doubt about it. She dress well – not like Kiwi and Aussie girls,' he snorted, 'but smart, you know.'

'Not a hair out of place,' I muttered, 'and squeaky clean, eh?' But the bartender had wandered off to serve another customer.

A middle-aged, red-faced American, who was chatting up a

25

plumpish Island girl several seats along, coughed and said, 'Say, I couldn't help overhearing what the bartender was sayin' to you. Tell me to mind my own business, if you will – but they were pretty weird customers who were hangin' about. One was a punk rocker, flamin' hair 'n' all, and the other was a pretty smart-looking broad, if yuh know what I mean. Straight outa beauty shop – string of pearls, black, tight-fittin' dress. Heard you say "squeaky clean" – sure, that pretty well describes her. I put her down as managin' the troupe.'

'What troupe?' I tried to sound bored and indifferent, to put him off, but he wasn't easily discouraged.

'Sure, they belong to a troupe – a band, or something, doin' a gig at Hotel Rarotonga, you know. Don't it beat everything – that fella in a frilly skirt! Gotta tell Camilla – she's havin' her hair done.' Having delivered that last piece of gratuitous information, he turned his attention once more to the girl, who was talking to the bartender, and showing not the slightest interest in him.

Having failed there, he turned his attention back to me. I could have done without it, because my thoughts were on the two demons, but he wasn't to be put off easily. He was an un-attractive individual, pushy, and with a red sweaty face, and wet lips, and it wasn't surprising the girl didn't take to him.

'What d'ya make of these Island broads? What she doin' here alone if she don't wanna pick up a guy?'

Was he drunk? I wondered, then ducked to avoid a cloud of alcoholic fumes heading straight towards me, then said hurriedly, 'Look, I'm sorry but I have a lot on my mind.'

'Oh, sure – sorry, pardner. By the way, call me Abe. You go ahead and don't mind me. I'd have a lot on my mind too, if a coupla freaks were after me – I sure would.'

The girl looked at him and frowned, then at me and smiled – and what a smile. It lit up a rather pudgy face and made it beauti-ful. She had a blunt nose with splayed nostrils, and intense black eyes, and from what I could see of her she had a nice figure, and she dressed simply in a *pareu*-style dress with green and yellow

26

hibiscus flower patterns. I could tell she looked after herself, and that her supple body was a matter of pride to her. Of course, now I recognised her! She was a well-known hula dancer from the Hotel Rarotonga. God knows what she was doing here, drinking gin and tonic at three in the afternoon! Had she fallen out with her lover? Who knows? Perhaps she only wanted to be alone in a motel where she was less likely to be recognised.

The American was talking to me and sounded peevish. 'You locals are sure a talkative lot. Pardon me for interruptin' yuh.'

'Sorry – what did you say?'

'I was talkin' to this broad here – '

'Not interested.'

Quite undeterred, he slapped a ten dollar note on the bar and said to the bartender, 'Another double whisky, sonny, and I think the lady would like her glass replenished.'

The young woman finished her drink, put her glass down, and walked out of the bar. She moved like a dancer, with elegant steps, and swaying hips, and every eye in the bar watched her go. She stopped in front of a unit, unlocked the door, and went in. So, she's a guest!

The American sighed and said, 'I coulda given her a helluva time. Camilla wouldna minded. She has her electronic keyboard thing to amuse her.' So that's the hideous sound I'd been hearing, I thought. 'Pity,' the American went on, 'the lady ain't buyin' today.'

'Or any other day,' I snickered. He was getting on my nerves.

'Oh, sure,' he said, and winked. 'Who is she, fella?' he asked the bartender.

'A dancer,' he replied. 'One of the best.' He wiped the bar disdainfully and moved away to serve another customer, the scrawny Kiwi, who I'd found out was an insurance salesman. He had won a week's holiday in Rarotonga for selling the most life policies in his area in the past year. God knows how he did it! He was a lugubrious fellow. Perhaps he scared his clients into insuring themselves.

I decided I wasn't going to hear any more about my tormentors, and was about to mosey back to my unit when the American said, 'This'll unglue you. I heard the punk rocker say to the dame, "I think I'll get a breast implant."' He laughed. 'Don't it beat everything?'

Back in my room, I lay on my bed and watched the antics on the ceiling of a pair of white lizards, while I tried to sort out the significance of what I had just learned. Sidewinder thinking of a breast implant! What could it possibly mean? At first I thought he must be losing his marbles, but, no, that couldn't possibly explain it. He had said it in the American's hearing, knowing that he would pass it on to me. And I didn't like the look in the American's eyes when he said it. They had glistened with malice.

I felt exhausted and baffled. Three years ago, I had lain in this room, watching perhaps the same lizards, and hearing the palm fronds above the roof, making a sound like rain, as they rustled in the breeze.

Then, of course, it struck me. Vanity! That's what it was all about. He liked himself so much in the role of a ballerina that he wanted to go the whole hog – *totus porcus* – and complete the transformation with a pair of phoney tits. He wanted to impress me – it was as simple as that. Then a bizarre phrase insinuated itself into my mind – 'cut and tuck, cut and tuck' – and I knew the fiend had put it there. He's capable of anything, but would he have the courage to have it done?

As I lay there in my underpants, while the electric fan spun noisily above me, I kept thinking of Bela's supple body – Bela, by the way, was the hula dancer's name – arousing myself so much I went and had a shower to cool off. The poet Auden writes somewhere of 'the sexy airs of summer', a phrase that perhaps applies more to the tropics, where it's summer all the time, than to anywhere else. Many a *papa'a* – my father included – has succumbed to their blandishments, and lived to regret it.

After my mother died, my father sought consolation in drink and sex, and I am reminded of the words of another poet when I remember once seeing my father sexually sated, lolling naked in his big double bed with two young girls, one of whom was my nanny. Island girls had a thing about being seen naked in those days, so my father's playmates were partly dressed. Anyway, on seeing me, they screeched, and made a grab for their clothes, while my father lay back and laughed.

You may know the passage in the *Cantos* where Pound writes of Circe's palace, or should I say piggery? – for that's what it was.

Girls talked there of fucking, beasts talked there of eating,
All heavy with sleep, fucked girls and fat leopards . . .

Well, when I think back to that occasion today, so embarrassing to a small boy, it's this passage that comes to mind.

I first saw Bela dancing at the Hotel Rarotonga, not long after it was opened. She wore a chaplet of green leaves and ferns through which her black eyes gleamed provocatively, as her rounded hips, shiny with sweat, swayed and swivelled to the hypnotic supplications of the drums. I have seen only one dancer superior to her, and that's Tia. But whereas Tia's dance was – dare I say it? – spiritual, Bela's appeal was earthy and direct.

There's a painting by, I think, Titian, of two lovely young women – one representing spiritual love is dressed, whereas the other representing earthly love is naked. This perhaps sums up the difference between Tia and Bela. Having said this, I may have given the impression that Tia is cold and aloof. Not a bit of it. In her own way, she dances as sexily as Bela, but perhaps more subtly. But, then, so she should, being the direct descendant of Kavariki, who, according to legend, invented the hula with the great *ta'unga* Urerua.

When Tia danced for me on our wedding night, in a natural *marae* of coral sand, surrounded by breadfruit trees and flowering shrubs, I wasn't the only one who wept, uplifted and carried away by the enchantment she created. The still night, the quiet sea, and the starry heavens entered her dance, and there wasn't one among us who didn't feel in some mysterious way privileged and blest.

Needless to say, Sidewinder felt miffed – he didn't like the dance one bit, and set out to destroy it. Lightning cracked viciously, thunder crashed and rolled, and down came the rain in dense blinding sheets. Hand in hand Tia and I rushed homewards, scooping up Tieki on the way. Tieki, by the way, is Tia's son by a former marriage. A sensitive spirited boy, loyal to his father, for months he resisted all my efforts to win him over. It was only in the past few months I felt I was making progress.

I was enjoying a late meal of cold chicken, salad, and raw fish, when I saw Bela walk into the restaurant. She nodded slightly when she saw me, stood still in the doorway, as she coolly surveyed the almost empty room, then came towards me, her swaying dancer's walk replaced by an honest down-to-earth stride. She had changed out of her *pareu* into an airy loose-fitting yellow dress, almost a mother hubbard. It took style to wear such a dress, and bring it off. I saw a number of heads follow her admiringly, and I felt boyishly proud when she stopped, and asked in a throaty voice, 'May I share your table? Or are you waiting for someone?'

'No – not at all,' I almost stammered. 'I mean yes – I'd love you to share my table. I've been a long admirer of your – '

'Are you sure?'

'Of course, absolutely.' What's wrong with me? I wondered. I'm almost stammering. It must be those naughty thoughts I had about her, that had made me take a shower. 'Look – I'm about to order a bottle of wine. Would you care to share it with me?'

'I'm not much of a drinker,' she said, as she sat down, with a dancer's sure grace. 'But I will have a glass of wine with you.'

Bela was delightful company. She was unaffected, simple, and straightforward. She had no pretensions whatever. She had learnt I was married to Tia, and wanted to congratulate me, and talk about her a little.

'We started dancing together,' she said. 'We went on many tours together, in the Pacific and the States. We were almost rivals – I should say we *were* rivals – but we remained good friends. Does she still dance?'

'Not professionally. She has a family to care for.'

'A pity. She was quite outstanding, you know.' Bela toyed with a spoon, and said, 'I don't know how to tell you this.' She caught my glance, held it for a moment, while she searched my eyes, as if uncertain what she'd find there. Then she looked away.

'Look,' I said, somewhat nervously, 'I'm a big boy now. I'm not afraid of the big bad wolf.'

She looked up quickly. 'So you know.' She hesitated, as if reluctant to continue, while I – well, you can imagine how I felt. My reference to the wolf had been flippant – I never expected it to be taken seriously. But I had unwittingly scored a bullseye, it seemed. While I looked blankly at her, speechless with dread, she asked more gently, 'You knew they were after you?'

'I've known for a long time.' Sweat was running freely down my back.

'The chief demon – ?'

'Sidewinder.'

'I know of no demon by that name.'

'It's what I call him.'

She smiled thinly. 'I see – but don't take him lightly. He's silly, but remember that the sillier a demon is the more dangerous he's likely to be, being unpredictable. And Sidewinder, as you call him, is as silly as a demon can be.' A smile, which she did nothing to conceal, played about her mouth.

'I don't take him lightly.' I found her concern reassuring. 'Are you a witch?'

'A *ta'unga*, yes – there are few of us left. I wish I could help you for Tia's sake – but I can do nothing without putting you in even greater danger. Sidewinder is immensely powerful, silly as he is – and his partner, Lamia, is almost his equal.' So that's her name, I thought. Didn't Keats write a poem about her? She's a snake demon, a worthy mate for Sidewinder. My God, what have I let myself in for?

31

Bela tossed her head in a girlish gesture, and I could see a dark mole behind her left ear, which could have been the source of her power, especially as it had sprouted black antenna-like hairs. She saw me looking in wonder at it, blushed, and brushed a lock of hair over it with her finger.

'I'm sorry – I didn't mean to be rude.'

'Now that you know my secret, promise me you'll tell no one – not even Tia. You could put me in great danger.'

'Your secret is safe with me.'

I don't know what got into me, but as we were leaving the restaurant I tried to chat her up. I have been faithful to Tia for three years – a considerable achievement for me, considering my earlier record of seductions and worse. I realised I had to change my destructive way of life, when mothers – so I heard – began warning their daughters off me.

Bela just stood there, looking at me and frowning a little, and then smiled and murmured, 'I don't think that's a good idea, do you? And I'm surprised – to put it mildly.'

I was beginning to shrink to the size of a walnut, when she went on to say, 'Don't think I'm not tempted. I could willingly hop into the sack with you – you're a handsome man. But you're married to Tia. She's my friend. I couldn't do it to her.'

All I could do was mumble, 'Forget I asked you. I wouldn't mind betting Sidewinder is behind it.'

Bela laughed. 'Nonsense! It's good old-fashioned lust. I felt it, too, but I had the good sense to suppress it. Don't look surprised. Women feel lust as men do. Even the nicest girl – perhaps I should say especially the nicest girl, from finishing school – feels lust.'

She looked at her watch and said, 'Goodness – look at the time. I must run. Thank you for a lovely evening – and please don't think I think the less of you for wanting to sleep with me. I feel flattered, but one has loyalties.'

CHAPTER THREE

WHAT HAPPENED TO mine? I brooded, as I watched her walk away. I almost slunk back to my unit, when who should turn up but the four-square manager, Miss Black. Had she witnessed my humiliation? I braced myself, fully expecting the worst, but it turned out she had news that drove my *faux pas* out of my mind.

'I have just heard on the news that a cyclone could be heading for your island. It's being buffeted by huge waves, and some houses have been blown down.'

I was appalled. 'Look,' I said, 'I've got to put a call through to Penrhyn straight away. Would the exchange be open?'

'It's open twenty-four hours a day,' she said, 'but I doubt if you'll get through now.'

'Maybe not – but I've got to try.' What an evening it was turning out to be, I thought, little knowing it was going to get worse, much worse.

'Shall I ring the exchange, and find out if you can get through?' Miss Black asked.

'If you wouldn't mind – I'm hopeless with mechanical things.' I have to admit I'm no good in a crisis. I tend to panic. My mind seizes up, leaving me in a fever of indecision. Tia is aware of my weakness, but loves me all the same. She may love me *for* my weakness. How could I think of betraying her?

A few minutes later, Miss Black broke into my thoughts. 'It's just as I suspected. There's no way of getting through to Penrhyn tonight.'

I thanked her for her trouble and returned to my room, confused and troubled. On top of the fiend, who really must be gloating now, I had Tia and all my people in Penrhyn to worry about. It was going to be a long night.

I made myself a cup of coffee, swallowed a couple of Amitriptyline tablets – yes, I'm still on them – and then dipped into Keats's *Lamia*. I always take a volume of verse with me when I travel, and this time it was Keats's 1820 collection, his greatest. Drowsy from the drug, I was about to put the book aside when I read Lamia's description. I immediately thought of Living Doll – not that the details fitted her exactly. She had a snake-like beauty, sinuous and flawless, but her tongue was black and stubby like a parrot's.

My mind couldn't take any more, and I drifted off into a deeply troubled sleep, in which I dreamt I was back in Penrhyn with Tia and was about to kiss her when she opened her mouth and out flickered a forked tongue that seemed to taste the air, before brushing my face. As I recoiled in horror, Tia giggled and said, 'How do you like the new me? Don't be surprised. We are all daughters of Lamia – we women.'

And all at once I was so overcome by lust I lost control of myself, and made violent love to her. My distaste for her oily body – it felt like soap – made me brutal, and I tried to hurt her, but all the time I was pumping her she called out ecstatically, 'It's the new me, the new me!' Finally, the climax came, my head blew apart, and she slid across the floor of what appeared to be a fish factory. It was covered in blood and scales. She came to rest against the wall in a tangle of coils, composed herself, and slid out of sight.

Was that Sidewinder shouting at me? I tried to open my eyes, but my eyelids seemed to be glued together. Breathing heavily, my nerves screaming in unison, I managed to open one eye, and gradually the fiend came into focus, still in his ballerina outfit. I remembered what Bela had told me, and I no longer considered it funny. There was someone else breathing heavily, apart from me. I raised myself on to one elbow and looked down the side of my bed, and saw Living Doll. She was glaring balefully at me, her legs tangled up in bedclothes. She was naked, and I wasn't so distraught that I couldn't appreciate the lustrous beauty of her body. She glowed from within, and was covered in light-green scales. Yes, she was the serpent of Keats's poem.

Sidewinder was laughing at me. 'You'll have to marry her now, and make an honest woman of her.'

'Can't,' I retorted, stupidly. 'I'm already married.'

'Yes, and to Tia. Wonder what she'll make of this *contretemps*. Not much, I'll wager.'

'You won't tell her, will you?' I was almost in tears. 'It will kill her.'

'I'm sure,' the fiend said smoothly, 'we can come to some mutually acceptable arrangement.' He fumbled about his person, and my heart sank, because I suspected he was looking for a contract form.

'Instead of exchanging pleasantries, I would appreciate it if one of you chums were to help me to my feet.' Living Doll sounded petulant and cross.

'Chums – yes,' murmured Sidewinder, approvingly. 'That just about sums up our friendship.' Now that he thought he had secured my soul he was prepared to be amiable. He looked fondly at me and whistled a merry tune. Then he reached down and helped Living Doll to her feet.

'My dear,' he murmured, sympathetically. 'You are scratched all over.'

'I feel as if I've been through a mincer.'

'Thanks very much.' I felt hurt. 'I didn't much like it, either.'

'There you are,' Living Doll snapped at Sidewinder. 'In future you can do your own dirty work.'

'What, sleep with *him* – not bloody likely.'

'I don't think you're much of a catch either,' I grumbled.

'Children, children!' shouted Living Doll.

'Look,' I shouted, 'why don't the pair of you bugger off? I've had quite enough of you for the night.' I knew I was asking for trouble, but I was so tired I didn't care.

'Look who's talking,' neighed Sidewinder. 'He tastes the fruits of her fair body, and then chucks her out. It's hardly decent.'

'It's indecent. I didn't enjoy it one bit. He scratches.' She raised an elegant arm for him to see.

'My dear chap,' said the fiend, sitting on the end of my bed, and looking half-sorrowfully at me. 'Have I ever been less than reasonable? You nod your head, but I know you don't mean it. Sure, we've had our differences – that's the nature of true friendship. Look at it this way. If I didn't care for you, would I bother to visit you as often as I do? Of course not. Look, I'm sorry about what happened tonight.' He leaned towards me and spoke in a stage whisper, that is, loud enough for Living Doll to hear. 'Listen to me, my friend. I tried to keep that woman off you, but she insisted – and there you are.' He ended lamely.

'You liar,' screamed Living Doll. 'It was your idea.'

'I don't care whose idea it was,' I shouted. 'I'm not signing anything.'

The two fiends stared at me and I stared back. It was an impasse. I felt I had won when Sidewinder let out a great groan and cried, 'I can't stand it! It's another of those staring contests,' and looked away.

I was delighted to see him looking so worried. He began mussing up his candy-floss hair, while his forked tongue flickered nervously. 'I say, old man, you really can't do this, you know. You've had your fun and now you must pay for it. And, for all we know, you may have got my colleague here in the family way.'

'It's the woman who always pays,' said Living Doll, tritely.

I stood my ground. 'I didn't invite her into my bed, so I don't see that I should pay.'

'But you did invite that strumpet Bela into your bed, didn't you?' sneered the fiend.

'Bela's not a strumpet – I mean, a prostitute – but I can tell you who is.'

'What's that supposed to mean?' snapped Living Doll. She didn't look beautiful now – tiny snakes were wreathing about her head.

'Just what I said.'

'Are you going to stand for that?' she yelped at Sidewinder.

'Oh, sit down, do,' he shouted. 'And get those things out of your hair – they give me the creeps.' She obliged with very bad grace.

'Now, then,' said Sidewinder, sternly, 'hand over your soul.'

I burst out laughing, and said, 'I can't hand over my soul like that. I wouldn't know how to go about it if I wanted to.'

'It's a teaser,' said Living Doll, concentrating hard.

'Well,' said Sidewinder, looking worried, 'what do we do now?'

'I have a suggestion,' I said. I could scarcely contain my glee. I had outwitted them. The game, but not the match, was mine!

'Oh, really,' said Sidewinder, looking hopefully at me. 'What is it?'

'You can bugger off.'

And that's what they did. I could hear them arguing all the way, his voice an angry rumbling, hers a dog-like yelping, until they gradually faded out of hearing. And good riddance, too.

I read awhile, and not my Keats this time, and was about to turn out the light when there came a discreet knocking on the door. I groaned, not them again! But the knocking persisted and I called out, 'Come in – the door's unlocked' – and who should enter but Bela, looking nervous and unsure of herself.

'Bela – is anything wrong?'

She stood beside my bed, saying nothing, until I murmured, 'What is it, Bela?'

'Oh, dear,' she said, with a nervous laugh, 'I shouldn't have come.'

'No,' I said, quoting her unkindly, 'it wasn't such a good idea.'

'I came because I felt you needed me. You looked so miserable when I left you tonight that I felt I had to come. I'm so stupid.'

'I did want you – or thought I did – but now I feel I've been run down by a bus. I'm not much good for anything, I'm afraid.'

'It was Sidewinder again, wasn't it?' She was sitting on the end of my bed, and it occurred to me that to an outsider we must have looked like a married couple having a bedside chat.

'It was, and he tricked me into believing I'd had sex with the snake demon – Living Doll.'

'And you didn't?'

'Of course I didn't. It was very cleverly staged – I'll give him that. He burst into the room like a jealous husband, claiming he had caught us in the act. He had done no such thing. Living Doll had arranged herself on Sidewinder's instructions; to give the impression that we'd made such passionate love she fell out of bed. No – don't laugh – it's true. I was caught in – what's the expression?'

'*In flagrante delicto.*'

'That's it – yeah.' But I didn't tell Bela that I'd had a disturbing dream in which Tia became a snake demon, but I had the feeling I didn't have to. She already knew.

What does that say about our marriage? I wondered, gloomily.

I must have wondered aloud, because Bela said, gently, 'Your marriage is safe – remember that.'

'It was another of Sidewinder's dirty tricks?'

'Yes.'

'It's the dirtiest of them all.'

Bela got up to go, and said, smiling sadly, 'This is the last talk you and I will ever have.'

'How can you say that? I feel I have made a new very special friend, and I don't intend to lose you.'

'You will remember me to Tia, won't you? I love her dearly.' She bent over me and kissed me, and I felt her tears on my cheek.

I was rudely woken next morning by loud voices outside my window, followed by rapping on my door. Still groggy from sleep, I croaked out, 'Come in – the door's not locked.' I expected the cleaning girl to enter with the change of linen, or the day's supply for the fridge, but in strode Miss Black, who looked bulkier and sterner than usual, to my not yet properly focused eyes.

She was followed by two policemen, the smaller of whom, the Sergeant, was a Penrhyn Islander, yet another cousin. He gave me a curt nod, as if to advise me he was on serious business, and said, 'We'd like a few words with you, sir.'

As I got out of bed and fumbled with my dressing gown, Miss Black excused herself and said to the Sergeant, 'I'll leave you to it, Tai,' and then gave me a withering glance, before sailing out.

'We may as well be comfortable,' I said. 'Take a seat, won't you. Would you like a cup of tea? I could certainly do with one.'

The policemen shook their heads, so I decided to do without one in the meantime, and sat on the bed. The second cop, who was built in the same mould as the manager, took out a notebook, and rumbled, 'We just wanna ask you a few questions, sir.' He moved his bottom into a more comfortable position. He was truly massive, and his face looked as if his maker hadn't kneaded out the lumps in it before declaring it finished.

My head was splitting, and I couldn't imagine what had brought two solemn cops to knock me up on what was clearly an official call. Then a horrible thought suddenly occurred to me, and I became wide awake. The cyclone – that must be it. Penrhyn had been hit and badly battered, with loss of life. Oh, no – the worst must have happened – Tia is dead!

Was it sympathy I saw in Tai's eyes? It must be true – Tia is dead! Tai and I played together as children, I remember. He was a serious little boy who never got into trouble, as the rest of us did, but he was not a toady or a prig.

'Is she dead, then?'

The two cops looked at each other, and I could see their interest quicken – then turned back to me.

'How did you know she was dead?' asked the big man. There was a glint in his eyes that I couldn't fathom.

So that's it, I thought. Tia is dead – and last night I had considered betraying her with her best friend. I loathed myself, even as I mourned Tia's death.

The policeman repeated his question.

'Well,' I said, collecting my shattered thoughts, 'I'd heard there was a cyclone heading towards Penrhyn and I assumed Tia must have been killed. What else could have brought you here? It can't be a social call, surely.' I groaned aloud. 'I wish you'd go away – you've done your duty.'

'Tia?' said the big man, looking questioningly at his Sergeant. I gathered he was the Inspector. 'What's he on about?'

'Tia is his wife, sir,' explained Tai, and then he turned to me and said, 'Take it easy. We don't come because of the cyclone, but on another matter. The cyclone it veered away before it could hit Penrhyn hard. Not much damage and no one killed. Your wife all right.'

'Thank God for that!' I had such a sense of relief I could have shouted for joy, but the Inspector's glowering look quickly brought me down to earth.

'Now then,' he said, surprising me, because I never expected a Polynesian cop to speak in the pompous tones of a vaudeville British cop. I looked at Tai and saw a definite twinkle in his black eyes. 'Now then,' the Inspector repeated, 'we want some answers from you, sir.'

'But I want a few answers myself,' I said, indignantly. 'You as good as told me a woman or a girl is dead. It isn't my wife, thank God, so who is it?'

The Inspector lowered his head and growled, 'We ask the questions, you will answer them. Now then, where were you last night?'

'Last night – that's easy.'

'Well?'

'I had a meal in the restaurant.'

'Here?'

'Yes. Look – what is going on?'

'You were alone?'

'No – I wasn't, as a matter of fact.'

'As a matter of fact,' he sneered, imitating my accent, which my enemies have unkindly described as *ersatz* BBC, 'tell us who you were with.'

'I was with Bela – you know, the dancer. Or rather she was with me. We had a meal together.'

'How well did you know Bela?' asked Tai, leaning forward as if to be in the right position to catch my answer.

'Did?' Bela was dead. I sat there stunned, unable to think clearly. Was it another of Sidewinder's doings?

'How well did you know her?' Tai was relentless. He was just doing his job, but for a moment I hated him.

'Not very well,' I stammered, and paused to collect myself. 'I have known her to speak to for, well, only a day, really.'

'Only a day, eh,' said the Inspector, heavily, 'but long enough so you could invite her to your room.'

'What are you trying to insinuate?' I disliked his tone of voice as much as the direction his interrogation was taking.

'Just answer the question.'

'I didn't invite Bela to my room.'

'We have people who will testify she was in your room until very late.'

'Well,' I said, indignantly, 'they're wrong. I repeat – I didn't invite Bela to my room.'

At this point, Tai interjected. 'But she was in your room, right?'

'Yes.'

'When did she leave your room?'

'I don't know – it must have been quite late.'

'You don't have a watch?' asked the Inspector, looking straight at the watch on my wrist.

'Yes, I have a watch?' I said, irritably jerking my wrist away, 'but I didn't look at it when she went out. If I'd known you were coming,' I said, sarcastically, 'I would have taken the trouble to note the time.'

'You didn't try to stop her leaving?' The Inspector was like a bulldozer. There was no way he could be stopped.

'Of course I didn't try to stop her leaving. Why would I want to do that – for Christ's sake?'

At this point, to my great embarrassment, I broke down, and burst into tears. I could see the two cops looking uncomfortably at each other, but the tears kept coming, and I blubbered like a child. Bela dead! I felt I'd lost a dear friend.

The Sergeant, who had been taking notes, fiddled with his ballpoint, while the Inspector averted his eyes, coughed, got heavily to his feet, and shambled out to the kitchenette ostensibly for a glass of water, but more probably for a quick nose around. He peered into the shower room, then filled a glass of water at the sink, and drank it. 'Hey, look at this,' he called out boyishly. 'There's a stain here just like a crab.'

'That's my talisman,' I said, smiling idiotically at Tai. 'I'm a cancerian.'

'You sick man, cuz,' he said, sympathetically. 'Too bad you got cancer.'

'There are a few questions I got to ask,' said the Inspector, coming back into the room, and sitting down again. He mopped his face and grumbled at the heat. His chair creaked as he shifted his bulk, and picked his teeth with a matchstick. The fan spun slowly above our heads, but brought little relief. Cries of pleasure were coming from the pool.

'I could murder a stubby,' grumbled the Inspector, smacking his lips.

'Have one on me,' I offered, brightly. 'I have a sixpack in the fridge.'

The Inspector was tempted, but he shook his head. 'No – we're on duty, eh, Tai?'

'Sure thing, Inspector,' said Tai, and cocked an ironic eye at me.

'Just a few more questions to wrap it all up,' the Inspector said, genially, 'and we get out of your hair, eh? You leave the restaurant at about nine-thirty – that's what the waitress say – and go straight to your room. Now Bela, where does she go?'

'To her room, I suppose,' I said. 'But I can't be sure.'

'You suppose? You don't follow her?'

'No, I tell you – I went straight to my room.'

'Did anybody see you go to your room? Think carefully. Did

42

you have a lot to drink – wine perhaps? Wine it goes straight to your head in the tropics.'

'As far as I know, nobody saw me go to my room – and as for the wine, I drank very little. Certainly not enough to make me drunk.'

The Inspector looked significantly at Tai, then turned back to me and said, 'Did I say you were drunk? Were you perhaps just a little drunk? Our warm evenings, they do strange things – make you forgetful, isn't that the truth, Sergeant?'

'Sometimes, sir.'

'For God's sake, Inspector. Bela and I shared a bottle. We certainly did not drink enough to be drunk.'

'Not you, perhaps, sir – but what about Bela?'

'She was perfectly sober.'

The Inspector thought awhile, and decided to change his tack. He studied my face, then said, 'What would you say if I told you that somebody saw you go to Bela's room?'

'I'd say,' I said, angrily, 'that he was a bloody liar.'

'He?' The question hung in the air.

'Well, whoever it was – he, she, or it.'

'OK, you were alone in your room. You had no visitors?'

I hesitated, which didn't escape him, and said, 'I had no visitors.' I couldn't mention the two fiends without the cops thinking I was crazy, and therefore capable of murder. It was now clear that it was a murder case they were investigating. The Inspector's eyes flicked from me to Tai, just as the door slammed with a shattering force.

'Shit – what the hell was that?' Tai jumped to his feet.

It was plain to me that Sidewinder was making his presence felt, and I smiled to myself, which I always do when the fiend loses his cool.

'The wind,' the Inspector said, calmly. 'A freak gust, but you find it funny. Murder isn't funny.' He sighed, took out another match, split the end of it with his nail, and began picking his teeth. 'I think we take him to the scene of the crime – what you say, Tai? Blood everywhere – on the walls, the bed, and on the victim. The killer stabbed her full of holes.' This formidable man looked piercingly at me and murmured, 'The killer – he must have been covered with blood. I look round your kitchenette and shower – no blood there.'

He groaned as he got to his feet, and then said to me, 'Come. I take you to the scene of the crime. You're a writer, Tai says. Well, here's good copy for your next book. Come.' And he stretched out a massive arm to gather me in and take me to the room where poor Bela was cruelly murdered. 'Come and see the room.'

'No, thanks, Inspector,' I said, trying to fight back more tears. 'Bela was a beautiful woman. I want to remember her as she was.'

'Suit yourself,' he grunted. 'Come on, Sergeant – we got work to do.'

'Oh, no, no, no! Tell me it's not true!' I will remember Tia's anguished cry as long as I live. I told her about Bela's death and her pathetic visit to my unit, but I couldn't tell her about my treachery.

'It's so horrible,' she wailed, 'and Bela was such a lovely person, too. You know we started dancing together, and travelled everywhere, giving performances. It's such a terrible loss. Do they know who did it?'

'If they do, they're keeping mum about it. Rarotonga is a small place, and I can't see the murderer getting away with it. I have a lot of time for the Inspector, whose name, believe it or not, is Erua Twinkelbaum – he's a great hulking man. But he's thorough. He gave me a thorough working over.'

'Surely, he didn't suspect you.'

'Tai – do you remember Tai?'

'He went into the police force, didn't he, and graduated at the New Zealand Police College.'

'That's the man – he's one of us. I played with him as a kid. He's the Sergeant in the enquiry. Anyway, he told me it's routine

44

to grill anyone connected in any way with the victim and eliminate them as suspects.'

'I wish you'd come home, darling. I hate the thought of your being caught up in anything as horrible as this. Please come home.'

'There's nothing I'd like better – you know that. But I must settle once and for all whether there's any way I can give you a baby.'

'Will you have to fly to New Zealand?' Poor Tia, she sounded quite forlorn!

'I may have to. I had hoped to talk to Dr Ruby, but I learned he's in Australia.'

'Dr Ruby?'

'You know – the Scottish doctor I tried to talk to by radio telephone a few months back.'

'I remember, darling. Didn't you say he was grumpy and not very helpful?'

'Yes – but I wasn't fair to him. It's impossible to discuss intimate things, with half the village listening. And the static doesn't help.'

'Did you hear about our cyclone?'

'Yes – I wanted to ring you.'

'We are fine. There was some damage – a few houses lost their roofs, and some trees were blown over, but no one was hurt.' I heard someone calling in the background. 'Must go, darling. That's Mama. Love you.'

There was a quiet knock on the door, and my immediate reaction was to groan, thinking the police had come back, but it was only the cleaning girl. She peered in the door, and I have to say that her presence was just the panacea that my spirits needed at the moment. Not even the murder, horrible as it was, could get her down.

She stood in the doorway, my bed linen over her arm, her eyes puffy from recent tears. 'I can't say good morning, 'cause it's not a good morning, is it?' Her voice was sad, but her natural cheerfulness kept breaking through. 'I do your bed now, or come back later?'

'Do it now.' I was drinking coffee and was about to ring Air New Zealand to book a seat for Auckland – but that could wait. I liked her bustling about, and I was curious to know the feeling in the motel about the murder.

'Oh, awful,' she said. 'All the girls they cry – they loved Bela. Miss Black too, she cries. She is worried that many guests won't come to stay.'

That figures! I thought. Still, she does have a lot to worry about. Guests could stay away in droves – initially, anyway, and that could cost the owners a lot of money.

'How are the guests taking it?'

'Not many come into breakfast today. The people they don't talk much, don't eat much either. They don't stay long eating. They drink their coffee and hurry away. I heard one man say to his wife, "We check out as soon as we get a flight to the States." Miss Black heard, and I could see she wanted to tell them not to go, but she just turn red and went into her office.'

'Have you heard if anyone has been charged?'

'People talk a lot – mention names – your name, too. That's all. We just staff – we know nothing.' Just then the manager called out her name. She sounded angry. The girl jumped, put down the linen, and hurried out.

I've been talked about! I didn't like that at all. It's no wonder a German couple, who had been friendly enough previously, looked at me oddly when I went for a walk soon after the cops had left me. Even then, rumours must have been flying around.

So much had happened to me in the short time I'd been in Rarotonga that I had largely neglected the main purpose of my visit. It had been disappointing to find that Dr Ruby was overseas, and as far as I knew there wasn't another doctor on the island with urological experience – so New Zealand it had to be. Another disappointment was to face me. I rang the Air New

Zealand booking office only to find all flights were fully booked for the week ahead. But there could be a cancellation, the girl assured me, so I gave her my name, the name of my motel, and the telephone number.

The girl pricked up her ears. 'Oh, isn't that the motel where someone was murdered last night?'

'Yes,' I replied, guardedly, 'but I'd rather not talk about it.'

'It was Bela, the dancer, I hear.'

'You'll ring me if there's a cancellation, won't you,' I said, and hung up, hoping my brusqueness wouldn't ruin my chances of an early flight.

A week to fill! What was I going to do? I was sure Sidewinder must have received the news with considerable pleasure, because the murder had created an atmosphere of fear and suspicion that he could exploit. A murderer was on the loose! Who would notice the dirty tricks of even an incompetent demon when there was the possibility of another killing. There could be a mass murderer out there! No – guests and staff would be so busy protecting their loved ones and themselves they'd have no thoughts for the victim of a demented fiend, such as me. As if in sympathy with the prevailing mood, the wind got up, the skies darkened, and before long heavy rain fell, lashing the ground as if to cleanse the world of its accumulated vileness.

CHAPTER FOUR

As BOLD AS you please, and sickeningly smug, who should slouch into my room but Sidewinder? He was still in his silly outfit and, if I were to believe what Bela had told me, still very dangerous.

'You might knock before you enter! It's not as if you're welcome!'

'Not welcome,' he said, uneasily, 'after our useful confabulation last night!'

'Useful confabulation, my eye!' I snorted. 'You have the cheek of Old Nick.'

He recoiled at that, and just the tips of his forked tongue appeared, but he recovered quickly, and the danger passed, with their immediate withdrawal. 'Don't speak disrespectfully of your betters,' he said, rather lamely. 'It's not healthy.'

'Is that a threat?'

'What does it sound like?' he growled. 'You need to be taught good manners.'

'That's rich,' I shouted, 'coming from someone with the cheek of a camel-driver! You crashed into my room last night – remember? – and demanded my soul.'

'I would have got it, too,' he grumbled, 'if that wretched woman had remembered to bring along the contract and a ball-point pen.'

'So you are blaming her now. Where's your loyalty?'

'Where's yours, matey?' he snarled. 'You put the hard word on Bela, and you have the gall to accuse me of disloyalty. I wonder what your dear Tia will think of that.'

'I was going to tell her,' I mumbled.

'Oh, you were, were you?' he said, sarcastically. 'You had a chance to tell her today. Why didn't you?'

'I had just told her of Bela's murder. I couldn't tell her in the same breath I had chatted her up. What kind of monster do you think I am?'

'Quite good – and learning fast. Tell you what. Why not ring her now? I'll give you moral support.'

'Moral support!' I exploded. 'What do you know about morality?'

'I know enough to recognise a hypocrite when I see one.'

'You bastard!' I said, looking for a bolt-hole. 'Tia has enough on her mind – and besides, she'll be busy preparing for the *tere* party.'

Sidewinder laughed nastily. 'I can teach you nothing.'

I'd had enough. I gritted my teeth, and walked towards him with my fists clenched, determined to sock him one, when he backed away, and would have turned tail and run, if I hadn't un- clenched my fists and said, wearily, 'You're not worth hitting. Why don't you fuck off now? I have enough on my plate without you on my back.'

Sidewinder was all sympathy. 'You do look tuckered out. Look – why don't you sit down, and I'll make a nice cup of tea. We still have a lot to chat about, and I do so like chatting with you.'

'I don't want a cup!' I shouted. 'I just want you to go.'

'You don't mean that. You're not yourself today. Making love can be so exhausting. Lamia, I mean Living Doll, can be so de- manding – and selfish. She thinks only of her pleasure.'

Sidewinder saw me clenching and unclenching my fists, and hurried on. 'Nobody can blame you for what happened. I don't and I'm sure Tia won't. It's all Lamia's fault. It was her idea to set you up, so you'd be caught *in flagrante delicto* – '

'I was *not* caught *in flagrante delicto*,' I protested. He was wearing me down. I felt listless.

'No, of course not. You know that, I know that. But there's no limit to the woman's duplicity. At this moment, she'll be going round Hell telling everyone she had trapped you with her femi- nine wiles. I blush when I think of what that woman did to you. To think that she put our friendship at risk! It's too bad. But I blame myself.' And the big phoney shook his head, and I saw a large tear roll down his cheek.

'My God,' I said, utterly disgusted, 'you take the cake!'

Sidewinder looked uneasily about him. 'Not that Name – please.' Then he hurried on. 'How could I do that to a tried and trusted friend? I should have known the woman was a liability. But I shouldn't be too hard on myself. I was only carrying out orders. I protested to my master – '

'You protested to your master,' I shouted, angrily. 'The responsibility was yours, you bastard. Don't try to sheet it back to your master – whoever he is.' I knew very well who he was.

The forked tongue flickered, menacingly. 'Take care,' he warned. 'My master is not to be mocked.' Realising that that wasn't the right tone, if he wanted to win me over, he coughed, and murmured, 'My master values your soul so much he'd give anything for the pleasure of – how shall I put it? – taking care of it. It would still be your soul, but we'd look after it. What could be more responsible?'

I exploded. 'Bullshit! You've gone too far this time. I'm going to kick you out on your ear, if you don't bloody well fuck off, you – you –' I was becoming incoherent with rage.

'No, wait,' he said, putting up his hand. 'Don't be impatient. Hear me out, won't you?'

'Look,' I said, 'I haven't time to listen to your drivel.'

He was offended. 'Not enough time. You have a whole week before you fly out.'

'Oh, you know about that, too.'

'You know my concern for you. I keep in close touch in case you need me if things go wrong.'

'I don't know what to say,' I said, sarcastically. 'Words fail me.'

'I don't want your gratitude,' he said, humbly. 'What are friends for?'

'I'd sooner be friends with a scorpion.'

'Oh, that *is* hard,' said the fiend, his voice actually breaking. 'But I forgive you, because I know you're not yourself today.'

'You know what you can do with your forgiveness, you can shove it up your – '

'Tut, tut,' he murmured, giving a playful shake of the head.

50

'We're having such a good talk. I really feel we are clearing the air at last. Let's not say anything we might regret.'

I picked up Keats's *Poems*, and pretended to read it. Perhaps if I ignored him, he'd get the huff, and go. But he just ploughed on, like one of those large oil tankers that take ten miles to stop after its engine has been turned off.

'Ah, Keats!' he enthused. 'A great poet, and I am so glad you've been reading *Lamia*. It describes our Lamia to a T. But let's not be distracted from our common purpose – to provide a home for your poor sick soul. No – don't look indignant. You haven't been looking after it, have you? You've been too busy chasing women, raping Lamia, and trying to seduce poor defenceless Bela, filling her with wine, and butchering her, when she turned you down.' His voice had risen to a shriek, reminding me of Hitler's hysterical speeches. I wasn't upset. I was appalled.

'You know,' I said, looking him straight in the eye, until he licked his lips nervously and looked away, 'you're mad – you've gone right off your rocker.'

'There's no need to be personal. I'm just doing my job. You will thank me one day.'

I was defeated. I was in flight. Nothing could stop this juggernaut.

Oh God, I thought, when he opened his mouth and began gesturing, he's started up again! But I didn't listen until he mentioned caretakers.

'You mean you see yourselves as caretakers of my soul? How very kind!'

'You think so?' He positively beamed. 'I thought you would.' He leaned forward confidentially and murmured, 'We're concerned for your health. You're still on drugs, aren't you? You're in no fit state to look after your health, let alone your soul. Let us look after it for you. Tia's no good at this sort of thing.'

I began to bristle. 'You keep Tia out of this.'

'Well, it's only my opinion, of course. No doubt she has many splendid qualities – even if she can't conceive.'

'You're twisting things around,' I shouted. 'I'm the one at fault.'

But the fiend was blocking his ears, pleading with me to keep my voice down. 'I didn't sleep too well last night. In fact, I didn't sleep at all.'

'No – you were too busy cooking up fiendish schemes!'

This tickled his sense of humour and he grinned broadly. 'What else can a fiend cook up, but fiendish schemes? It stands to reason.' He winked at me, and murmured, 'Dear boy!'

He then smiled fondly at me, shook his head, and said quite earnestly, 'You know – we've had so many happy hours together. Let's not spoil things now. Let's not shout at each other.'

Sidewinder leaned towards me and stretched out a scaly claw that filled me with revulsion, but he took no notice. He must have been confident he had me in his power, because he didn't withdraw it as he would normally have done.

'Listen, my friend, as long as you are on drugs you are a danger to yourself. We want to be in your corner, when the big fight starts – '

That made me sit up. 'What big fight?'

He frowned and said, 'I'm talking metaphorically. You are supposed to be a writer. Not a particularly good one, if you want my opinion.' He heard me swear under my breath, and hastily apologised. 'Of course, I didn't mean that.' He sighed and said, 'Now where was I?'

'You in your small corner – ' I sang.

'And I in mine.'

He twinkled at me. 'So you went to Sunday school. It doesn't seem to have done you any good.' He just couldn't resist the opportunity to insult me.

'What do you know about Sunday school?' I grumbled. 'It's hardly the place you'd expect to find a fiend.'

'Precisely,' he laughed. 'Catch them when they're sprats, and they're yours forever.'

He saw I wasn't laughing, and at once composed his face. 'Let's get down to business,' he said, briskly, 'and wrap it up. You may not believe it – '

'I won't.'

'I shall ignore that. You may not believe it, but we are concerned with the health and safety of your soul. Won't you consider entrusting it to us for safekeeping? It would be terrible if it fell into the wrong hands.'

You could have heard me laughing a mile away, I'm sure. I laughed and laughed until I fell helpless on my bed. I clearly upset my next-door neighbour, because he began to thump the wall and curse loudly.

'Now, you've done it,' the fiend whispered. 'There's only one further point I wish to make.'

'Well, say it – and get out.'

'Do you know how many souls we have in our keeping?'

'I don't know, and I don't bloody well care.'

'Oh, you should, dear boy, you should – because very shortly your soul will be joining them. And do you know – everyone is grateful to us, and I know you will be, too.'

I'd had enough. I picked him up by the scruff of the neck and the back of his stupid frilly skirt, which tore, and turfed him out, narrowly missing the German couple. And did he yell! It was music to my ears.

I then collapsed exhausted on my bed, and for once fell into a deep and dreamless sleep. I was again woken by the sound of knocking, and I called out, furiously, 'Go away – damn you, and let a fellow sleep.' I thought I heard whispering, then the sound of footsteps walking away. 'Good riddance!'

Who was it this time? I wondered idly. It couldn't have been the fiend, surely. He'd be somewhere, licking his wounds, or sending a message back to his master, no doubt giving him the impression I was about to crack. He once told me he had repeatedly been denied promotion, and that I was his last chance. He implied it would be mean and petty for me not to participate in drawing up a report on his progress.

When I laughed and said, 'What progress?' he just looked hurt.

'Participate' was the buzz word in Hell, he told me, and many of his associates had earned high grades because their victims had been fully cooperative. When I questioned his choice of the word 'victim', he smiled shyly, and said he was using the word in its special sense. Victims in Hell, he explained, are graduates who got high grades for their contribution to their own damnation. They achieved this by remaining positively evil during their trials on earth, and by helping their tormentors in every way. They did this by revealing every vileness they had thought or committed – and, of course, they were graded high or low according to the vileness of the thought or deed, and the degree of suffering it had caused.

A really vile deed, such as raping and killing an old woman or a child, would earn high marks, while a relatively 'minor aberration' – the fiend's choice of words – such as blasphemy, scored a correspondingly low mark.

'I find that surprising,' I objected. 'I would have thought that blasphemy was one of the great sins.'

He smiled gently at me as a mother might smile indulgently at a child who is mentally retarded. 'Of course, it is – in your world, but down below we have different values. The more you curse You Know Who, the fewer marks you score. We don't want YKW to think He's important down below.'

'I find that confusing and contradictory. I just don't get it.'

'Of course not – you aren't meant to. We can't have logic in Hell. 'Enlightenment' is a dirty word to us, while 'obscurantism' is a good word. We have many politicians who are respected members of our community.'

'You mean victims.'

'If you like. You see – the beauty of evil is that it's so simple that even idiots can do well. They don't need a crash course, or a university degree – although that helps. It's beautifully simple.'

'You mean simply stupid – like that outfit you're wearing.'

I thought I'd get a rise from him, but he smiled indulgently, and murmured, 'We'll win you over yet.'

My God, the knockers are back! The door is positively thundering.

I heaved myself off the bed, and shuffled to the door, groaning. 'All right, all right I'm coming.' I swung it open, and the German couple almost fell into the room.

'Jesus Christ, what do you want?'

'Dere's no need to blaspheme,' spluttered *mein Herr*.

It suddenly dawned on me who he was. 'You're Siegfried's brother, aren't you?' Siegfried was an old drinking crony whom I used to see in the Banana Court, the town's main waterhole. His wife used to beat him up for no apparent reason, but the more she beat him the more devoted he became. He fell off his chair in the bar one day and died – the coroner said of cardiac arrest, but I think his wife had hit him once too often. So, here was his brother, a dead spit of him, but as yet an unknown quantity.

The couple just stood there, staring at me. The woman had a heavy occluded jaw, a square face, a thin red nose with a white tip. I couldn't help thinking she'd be more than a match for the redoubtable Miss Black. Her husband was small and plump, with a white pointed beard, a bulbous nose pitted like a strawberry, and bushy eyebrows. He had an egg-shaped body like his brother's and similar stunted legs.

'What can I do for you?' I asked, looking from one to the other.

'Harumph,' said the man, tugging at his beard, so that his chin came down, and he looked at me through the thickets of his eyebrows.

'Excuse, please. Ve vant to ask a favour ov you, my vife unt I.'

Oh, Lord, I thought, I've got to stop him at all costs, or he'll drone on interminably and unintelligibly. But how can I do that without giving offence? And how can I stop the woman's eyes from seeing right into my soul?

'Look,' I said, looking pointedly at my watch, 'I have a lot to do, and I'm afraid I can't spare the time.'

'We won't take up much of your precious time,' said the woman, sourly. 'Five minutes are all we need. Surely you can spare us that.'

Well, at least she can speak reasonable English. It could be quite interesting, and a writer is always looking for copy. I opened the door wide, and said, 'Come on in.'

You should have seen the woman's eyes glisten, as they took in the disordered bed, the humped up pillows, the crumpled sheets at the foot of the bed, and the soiled towels lying in a heap in a corner. The thin white tip of her nose quivered and I swear a bead of moisture appeared and hung there, and just as it fell, out flicked her tongue and caught it. Her jaws clicked as she closed her mouth.

'What can I do for you?' I asked, shaken by the thoroughness of her survey. 'Do sit down.' I cursed the cleaning girl under my breath for not coming back and tidying up.

She looked sourly at the chairs on which my clothes – and to my embarrassment a pair of pink knickers – were draped, and muttered, 'No, thank you. We'd prefer to stand.' Another dew-drop was forming on her nose, and again her tongue flicked out, caught it, and withdrew.

'Ich vill zit town,' said the man, earning a glare from his wife, 'sank you.' I was surprised to see him twinkling at me, and I twinkled back. 'My tear, vy don't you zit down.'

His wife looked distastefully about her, and didn't reply.

'As you vill,' he said, good-naturedly. 'Shall I talk or you, my tear?'

'I'll do the talking, Erik,' she snapped. 'You'd take a month of Sundays.'

'A month of Zundays,' he chuckled. 'Zis is a shtrange language zis English!'

That nose! I thought – I won't be able to keep my eyes off it. And the tongue – it seems to have a life of its own. Like a ferret in a hole!

'Now, then,' said the woman sternly. 'We have a bone to pick with you. We have reason to believe that the transvestite who's been hanging around is a friend of yours.'

Here it goes again, I thought wearily. What's Sidewinder been up to now? He's certainly a sight for sore eyes! What's old Erik think about it? I looked across at him, and was surprised to see him wink at me. He seemed a decent enough old codger, so I winked back.

'It's a disgrace,' the woman went on, her mouth tightening, as she observed the wink. 'I complained to the police, but they said they were too busy with the murder enquiry to chase away lunatics.' She snorted. 'These people have no idea how to run things. Are they competent to run their own country?' She looked sternly at me, another dewdrop forming. 'Well – what are you going to do about it?'

'What can I do?' I shrugged. 'He's not my responsibility.'

'Well, you can at least get him to put on sensible clothes, and get his hair attended to. He's an eyesore – a freak.'

'Well,' I said, with a laugh, 'he's a bit of a clown, but quite harmless, really.' Wait for it, I told myself, and sure enough there was an angry thump on the roof.

Erik frowned and looked up, but his wife seemed not to notice. 'He's a blot on the landscape,' she said, concluding her diatribe with an angry nod directed at her husband, who smiled amiably.

'He's worse than that,' I murmured. 'He's a demon.'

Wow! You should have seen her change! I could almost hear her mind click like a calculator, as she recognised the truth of what I was saying, and for once that long tongue forgot its duty, and the dewdrop fell unregarded on the back of her hand.

She's a witch! I knew that with absolute certainty, and when I looked across at the man he was nodding at me, and smiling.

'Sank you,' he said, giving me a little bow, and following his trembling wife out the door.

It wasn't the last I would see of this remarkable couple.

It had been a busy morning – first, the police, then Sidewinder, followed by the German couple.

I hadn't worked on my novel since I left Penrhyn, and as I had an hour to fill before lunch, I took out of my briefcase the chap-

57

ter I'd been working on. I read it through, made a number of corrections and minor changes, and then rewrote the final page, which had given me a lot of trouble. Then I read it through again, and crossed it all out. It wouldn't do. I couldn't concentrate on it, so I put it aside.

Perhaps Air New Zealand had received a cancellation. I rang the booking office and the same girl answered as before. I asked her if any cancellations had been received.

'I'm afraid not, sir,' she said. 'What was your name again?'

I told her. 'Oh, yes, you live at the motel where Bela was killed. How dreadful!' I heard her shuffling some papers, and then she said, brightly, 'I'm afraid no cancellation has been received. But I do have your name and telephone number, sir, and I shall ring as soon as a cancellation has come to hand.'

I thanked her and hung up. I mooched about, and finally picked up my Keats, and thumbed through *Lamia* again, and wondered how he had managed to describe her so accurately and vividly:

Her head was serpent, but, ah, bitter sweet!
She had a woman's mouth with all its pearls complete . . .

Yes, that describes the perfection of Living Doll's teeth. Did Lamia appear to Keats, as she had to me, in the shape of a young, not so warm-blooded, and beautiful woman. I thought of Fanny Brawne and the anguish of Keats's relationship with her. Did Lamia take her shape only to play fast and loose with his emotions, reducing him to a bundle of hysterical appeals and accusations?

As to his extraordinary letters – only a lover who had slept with the snake demon could have written them.

Miss Black gave me a cool reception in the restaurant, and led me to one of the less favoured tables. I don't think she had a snitch against me; it's just that she liked to give every table a turn, for it upset her that some tables were spurned merely because they happened to stand in a draught, or had their view blocked by a pillar, or were too close to the swinging door that led to the kitchen. She could hardly be described as tender-hearted, but she did have a soft spot for the inanimate, as I confess I have, especially for stones. A soft spot, incidentally, that I share with Goethe, who was known to talk to stones.

Anyway, I took my seat and waited to be served. I had noticed that my entry had caused a number of curious heads to turn in my direction, then draw together in whispered tittle-tattle. The young waitresses also whispered among themselves, reluctant to serve the suspect the police had questioned in regard to Bela's murder. But a slap by Miss Black sent one of them skittering to my table.

I put in my order, and as I waited I looked about me. There was nobody among the diners to interest me, so I looked at the local newssheet that I'd picked up at the desk. The murder had been given prime position on the front page. I skimmed through it, but found nothing that I didn't already know. There was a blotchy photograph of Bela, arms aloft and smiling, as she swayed in a hula. I couldn't bear to look at it, and think how brutally such a lovely woman had met her end.

I was drinking coffee and nibbling biscuit and Tararua cheese when I looked up and saw Abe, the American, bearing down on me in bright yellow pants and an iridescent shirt, *University of Hawaii* scrawled across the front – a ghastly sight!

'Say – do ya mind if I join ya? Sure would like a word.'

I sighed. 'Go ahead – take a seat.' But I continued reading the paper, making it clear to him that I accepted him on sufferance. I didn't like him, so I didn't see why I should put myself out to satisfy his curiosity. I assumed he wanted to know about the grilling the police had given me.

'Some rag, ain't it?' He poured himself a cup of my coffee.

'Do help yourself,' I said, sarcastically. I folded my paper and put it beside my plate. 'Well, how can I help you?' I knew I sounded pompous, but pushy people like Abe always put me on the defensive. I find it hard to be rude and brush them off – it's not in my nature, worse luck. So, I allow myself to be put upon and, worse, to be bored silly.

'Things are hotting up,' he said casually. 'I think the cops are closing in on their man.' He helped himself to my biscuit and cheese. 'Give ya a hard time, did they, the fuzz?'

'No, as a matter of fact, they didn't.'

He munched away noisily, head down, and looking at me from under his eyebrows, biscuit crumbs falling from his lips. He had bits of white at the corners of his eyes which, quite frankly, I found disgusting.

'Don' worry about it. They got nuttin' on ya.' He leaned towards me, his breath enveloping me in a mix of stale Jim Beam and aftershave, and muttered, 'I'd put my dough on the Kiwi Kid.' He laughed. 'Yep – that's who my money's on.'

'The Kiwi Kid,' I said, trying to get up courage to walk out. 'Don't think I know him.'

'Sure ya do – the kid with the acne problem.'

'His old man's an insurance salesman?'

'Bullseye. The old guy's nearly outa his tree with worry, 'cause the kid's flown – like a dicky bird.'

Abe's language was curiously dated, as if he'd been influenced by watching too many late-night movies, perhaps Bogart or George Raft. He leaned towards me again, and I was inclined to duck. 'I hear you bin arst not to leave the island. Don' take it ta heart. It's just a precaution.'

I didn't bother to correct him, because I knew he was just fishing, and I wasn't about to give him satisfaction by rising to the bait.

He looked up at me rather sourly, as I got to my feet. 'The Kiwi Kid's our man. Ya better believe it.'

Had the kid actually run away? I wondered as I walked back to my unit. Or is it just a yarn that Abe had made up to attract attention? When I reached my door I was surprised to see it open.

It must be the cleaning girl, I thought, but another surprise awaited me when I entered and saw Inspector Twinkelbaum seated in my chair, his vast bulk seeming to overflow it.

'How nice to see you quite at home in my room,' I said, sarcastically. 'I suppose you had a good nose around.' I was more worried than I sounded. Perhaps Abe is right. Perhaps I am a suspect.

He got heavily to his feet and apologised for taking the liberty. 'I couldn't resist it,' he said, lamely. 'The door was open and in I went. I wanted to have a quiet word with you. I look all over the place and I see you in the restaurant, so I thought that if I waited I would catch you here. No, sir, I didn't nose around, as you put it. I just sit and wait.'

That will be the day! I thought. But aloud, I said, 'Bully for you, Inspector.'

'What was that?'

'It's just an expression. Well, what can I do for you?' This was fast becoming an overworked expression.

'You have plans to fly to New Zealand?' he said, watching me closely.

'That's right – as soon as I can get a cancellation. But I suppose you knew that already.'

He ignored my heavy sarcasm, merely saying, 'I ask you not to leave the island in the meantime. We may need to speak to you again. Do I have your word?'

'Sure – why not?' I tried to sound casual, but my mind was seething like a cauldron. My God, that bloody fool Abe was telling the truth! 'I suppose you'll have men watching the airport and the wharves.'

He wasn't amused. 'You will have your little joke.'

CHAPTER FIVE

THAT AFTERNOON I was waiting by the motel office, hoping to
speak to Miss Black, when a taxi drew up outside. It was an old
Ford, brown with a yellow roof, and rusty as are many of the cars
on the island. Such cars, as one wag put it, are hopes held together by rust. A Chinese couple got out, and then – would you
believe it? – Fat Boy himself got out. And equally surprising, the
driver was my old shipmate Muscles, who gave me a warning
look, then opened the boot, and began unloading. What was that
all about? That look, I mean.

I mentioned Muscles earlier and said a little about him, and I
wondered then whether I would run into the fourth occupant of
my cabin, Fat Boy himself. Well, here he was chewing on a
chicken leg, the rest of the bird sticking out of his coat pocket.
He seemed to be in what I can only describe as a feeding daze.
He had grease on his chin, around his mouth, and on the tip of
his squashy nose, but he had presence of mind to recognise me,
and smile – and a remarkably sweet smile it was.

Paradise Lost was my reading for that voyage, and I was interested in what Milton had to say about Beelzebub, little knowing
I'd be running into him in Penrhyn. Feeling tired, I picked up an
old magazine and read about some nutcase in the States who bet
he could eat an entire car, and when his bet was taken up, set
about devouring it, bit by bit, beginning with the nuts and bolts.
It took some time, the article said, but in the end he ate it all,
and won his bet. I didn't believe the article, thinking it was some
kind of legpull, nor did the other passengers, except Fat Boy who
was so interested he actually stopped chewing.

That night, after taking more tablets of Amitriptyline than was
good for me – I had been going through a severe patch of de-
pression – I fell asleep and had an extraordinary dream. I dreamt

that we had struck a reef and, as the ship was foundering, Fat Boy, grown huge as Goya's *Giant*, broke pieces off and stuffed them into his mouth, and even as we were struggling in the water, he devoured what was left – the masts, the rigging, and finally the crow's-nests. I had a grudging respect for Fat Boy after that.

It's absurd, I know, but I actually suspected him of being one of the demons on board, who were giving me a bad time. It didn't seem possible that any human being could eat so much, but with a demon it's a different matter. A demon can eat up to his weight in unshriven Christians on a Black Sunday – as the saying has it – and as Sidewinder confessed to me once, an unshriven Christian is not nice to eat. Anyway, Fat Boy always turned up just as the sound of whistling was fading out. And, as is well known, the Devil himself always announces his presence by whistling. So, if you hear in the dead of night a whistle that seems to come from nowhere, beginning on a wheedling low note and rising to a high, almost cheeky, note, take care: Old Nick himself may be about to pay you a visit.

'Have you just flown in from Penrhyn?' I asked him.

'That's right,' he said, in a surprisingly squeaky voice for such a big man. Apart from the calibration flight, a weekly service had recently started up. I could have waited for a flight on it, but I was impatient, and anyway the calibration flight is cheaper.

'Cost Tia a lot of money.'

'What was that?' I couldn't believe my ears.

'That's right – Tia paid my fare.' He nibbled the last bit of flesh from the chicken bone, while I looked on, the ground rocking underneath my feet.

'I don't believe you,' I told him. 'You're having me on.'

Fat Boy casually tossed the chicken bone to a pathetic half-starved stray with micky mouse ears that was always hanging round the motel. He pressed the back of a pudgy hand to his mouth, burped loudly, and continued stuffing himself with the rest of the chicken. I felt like shouting at him, 'Stop eating, for Christ's sake!' but he probably wouldn't even notice.

'Tia she worried about you. So she sent me to Raro to guard you.'

'What are you talking about?' I couldn't understand why Tia hadn't consulted me before taking a step that was both costly and pointless. I didn't need a minder – certainly not an overweight clown like Fat Boy. 'Guard me – I don't need guarding!'

'Tia she think you in danger, and she send me to look after you,' he said calmly, and took out a black handkerchief and began wiping his face. He must have noticed I had no faith in him, but bore me no illwill.

He chewed away on the last of the chicken, tossed it to the dog, licked his fingers, and said, 'I guard you good – you not worry. I got Black Belt. I keep you safe.'

Safe from what? I wondered. As I think I've mentioned earlier, Tia has never given any clear sign she's aware of Sidewinder and his persecution of me. So, if Sidewinder wasn't the cause of her worry, who, or what, was? I didn't like to think.

Moreover, Tia must have paid for the flight out of her small nestegg, which her former husband had settled on her when their marriage broke up. I had assumed she was keeping it for Tieki's education in New Zealand, and I was disappointed that she had chosen to spend so much on what seemed to me an unnecessary precaution and expense.

Well, Fat Boy was here now, and I suppose I had to see to his accommodation. The unit next to mine was vacant, and after I had arranged it with Miss Black Fat Boy was soon in residence. I watched him settle in. He unpacked his bag, then kneeled, and squeezed into the small fridge a huge slab of tuna that he had brought from Penrhyn. Whatever happened, he wasn't going to starve. Then he got slowly to his feet, pushing his great weight up by straightening his legs, and slumped into a chair, and wiped his streaming face with his sleeve.

He looked at me out of small cunning eyes, sunk in fat. 'You think me greedy – is that not so? I eat a lot – sure, but I a big man, must keep up strength, like super-heavyweight lifters. Like them, my strength it is in my belly. I show you.'

He got up, took off his shirt, thumped himself on the belly, and said, 'Punch me – go on.'

'Must I? Don't know if I can do that.'

'Go on – take a swing.'

'Oh, all right.' I closed my fist and hit him, pulling back a little.

'Harder – much harder.'

I punched him again as hard as I could, and the huge belly that seemed so much lard was like a steel drum.

I left him swaying in front of the mirror, both arms raised and bent in the classic Charles Atlas pose, and admiring his bulging biceps. But I hadn't gone far when I remembered I hadn't locked my door, and I was about to pass his open door to get to mine when I thought I heard a familiar voice. Those unctuous tones were unmistakeable. It was Sidewinder, by God! But what was he doing in Fat Boy's room?

I didn't know what to do. Fat Boy was in terrible danger. Sidewinder was in his room, and there was nothing I could to save him. When I heard a squeal of laughter that could only be Fat Boy's I knew – what I should have known all along, and had indeed suspected on board ship – that my minder Fat Boy was a demon. Now Sidewinder was also laughing, or rather giggling, and even in my terror I wondered if the demon had chosen a laugh like this as being appropriate to one in a frilly dancing skirt.

Then they both fell silent, and I knew they were aware of my presence, and were listening intently. And although the sun shone brightly and the coconut palms swayed and rustled above me, evil emanated from the room through the open door. It flowed around me and drew me ever closer to the room where the two fiends were waiting.

It was Miss Black who saved me. She saw me as she was showing the Japanese couple to their unit. She was surprised, as she told me later, to see me apparently sleep-walking in broad daylight. She had heard that it was dangerous to wake a person in that state, so she had led me to my room, helped me into a chair, waited until I came to, when she reverted to her normal efficient and domineering self.

'You've had too much sun. I'm surprised at you, a grown man. You should know better.' Then she made me a cup of tea, waited until my hand was steady enough to hold it, then left me with the warning to keep out of the sun meanwhile and to take better care of myself.

What of the two demons? When I had fully recovered from my shock, I went next-door, and surreptitiously tried the door-knob. It was locked. I looked through the window. The room was dark and unoccupied.

Later, I asked at the office if anyone answering Fat Boy's description had checked in. No one had. So what was Sidewinder playing at? Had Fat Boy replaced Living Doll/Lamia who seems to have been recalled? I never saw Fat Boy again. Can you wonder why I am confused?

Fat Boy's arrival had been a distraction – and, finally, an unpleasant one. So, I returned to the office, looking to complete what had taken me there in the first place. I wanted to talk to Miss Black about my father. I have mentioned that my father had beaten hers for the job of resident agent in Atiu, but not that they had been rivals in many activities since their school days.

I knew my father was broken-hearted when my mother died, and began to drink heavily and chase women, or, rather, and more accurately, he didn't discourage the bold hussies who wanted to replace my mother, and thought the best way of accomplishing that was to hop into his bed. He was then forty years old, still lean and handsome, and being a *papa'a* with money in the bank, he was an irresistible lure for any young woman lucky enough to capture him. I remember an old salt, who had sailed with father, telling me that two high-born Atiuan girls had scrapped over him, but were quickly married off by their respective families.

Miss Black at last came out of her office, and was surprised to see me waiting. 'Are you well enough to be up and about?' she asked, looking closely at me. 'You still look pale.'

'I'm all right,' I muttered. A couple of guests had come into the lobby, and one of them, a loud Aussie grazier, had cornered me in the bar the night before, and tried to pump me. I slid off my bar stool and sloped off, without replying.

'Yo'K, mate?' he called out, then dug his companion in the ribs with his elbow, and muttered something I couldn't catch.

'Sure,' I called back. 'Why shouldn't I be?'

'Good on, yuh.' Then both porky men, bellies hanging over their technicolor shorts, weaved their way in the direction of the bar.

Miss Black turned from a guest with whom she had been chatting, and murmured, 'What was that all about?'

'I wouldn't know,' I muttered, and hurriedly changed the subject.

'What did you want to see me about?'

'I thought you might fill in some blanks in my father's life.'

She bristled. 'Why would I want to do that? I know many Island girls flung themselves at him – the handsome hunk! – but I wasn't one.'

Just as well, I thought, looking at her solid figure.

She caught my glance, and scowled at first, then broke into laughter. 'It would take a big man – a front-row forward – to catch me.' She looked at her watch, grimaced, then said, 'Come into my room where we can talk without being interrupted.'

She led the way into a small room adjoining the office, where there were several chairs, a divan, a drinks cabinet, but not much else.

'Care for a drink,' she said, going to the cabinet.

'No, thanks.'

'Mind if I have one?'

'No – go ahead.'

She poured herself a small sherry, sat down facing me, and said, 'Well, what can I tell you?'

'You told me that my dad did yours out of a job that he thought he should have been given, and he hated my dad ever after.'

'Did I say that?' She pressed the bridge of her glasses, and stared owlishly at me. 'I suppose I must've – more or less.'

'Well,' I said, warming to my theme, 'I can understand a man being bitterly disappointed. But our fathers – so I gather – used to be such good friends. It seems to me that your old man's hatred for mine was out of all proportion to what is supposed to have started it. I understand that even your family was dragged into it, and developed a healthy hatred for mine. Something else must have happened. I'd like to know what it was.'

Miss Black took off her glasses, making her eyes look strangely vulnerable, breathed on them, cleaned them with a cloth, then put them on again. At last she spoke, a slight tremor in her voice. It was an unusual experience to see this formidable woman nervous.

She looked at me, and sighed. 'Yes – there was something else. I will tell you providing you promise never to reveal what I tell you.'

'I promise.'

'Very well.' She collected her thoughts and said, 'I only discovered it by chance when I was going through my father's papers – he's been long dead, of course. It was some scribbled notes, concerning a young very beautiful girl. I remember her vaguely. Your father and mine loved her dearly. It was absurd, I suppose – a sort of delayed adolescent crush.'

'Was this before our fathers married – or after?'

'Oh, after, of course. They used to call on her, and make a lot of fuss over her. It was pretty innocent and, I suppose, silly. Middle-aged men often make fools of themselves over young girls.'

'Where did they, as you say, call on her?'

'Oh, at her home – it was all above board. It wasn't a sneaky thing, not then. Her parents were usually there, kids running round – that sort of thing. But your father wasn't happy with this arrangement. To put it bluntly – he wanted her for himself.'

That sounds like Papa, I thought, bitterly.

Miss Black flicked her eyes at me, as if she had read my thoughts. 'He wanted her all to himself,' she repeated, bitterly.

'Well, to cut the story short, he got her pregnant, she had a diffi-cult birth, complications set in, she lost a lot of blood, her blood pressure fell and never recovered – and the poor girl died – and the baby did, too.'

I don't know how long I sat there, stunned, and unable to think clearly, but something stirred in my mind, some vaguely perceptible key to the troubles I had been experiencing since my breakdown and subsequent persecution by Sidewinder.

Miss Black was helping herself to another sherry. She turned and said, 'Sure you won't have a drink?'

'I want to go and be by myself for a while.' I sighed deeply. 'I have a great deal to think about.'

'Your father,' she murmured, as I was about to leave, 'wasn't a very nice man.'

What sort of man was my father? I realised I really didn't know. I was a small boy when he died, and I remember him as a rather forbidding presence rather than a loving father – not that he was ever harsh. On the contrary, he was always genial and kindly in a bluff hearty way, such as one imagines an uncle ought to be. He was undemonstrative, and didn't like being touched, except per-haps in love making – but I know nothing of that.

He was reserved even stiff in manner, if he didn't like or approve of the company he happened to be in. He was most at ease in the company of his drinking mates, some of whom were *papa'a* layabouts, and some Penrhyn men, relatives of Tia, who had found jobs in Rarotonga. He didn't particularly like the illegal orange beer, brewed in kerosene tins in the bush, and drunk when the imported New Zealand beer had run out, being a whisky man himself, but he drank it to be companionable and to be one with the Islanders.

That old salt, I mentioned earlier, told me of these binges – which is what they quickly became. 'Regular hooleys, they were,' he said, his eyes lighting up. 'Those Island girls – they sure could give you a good time. They kept up with the men, and even out-drank them. One moment, we'd be a bunch of jokers, men and girls, getting shicker on orange beer, and the next, every blessed soul had disappeared – paired off and disappeared into the bush. The administration knew about it, and tried to stop it – the drinkin' and all. But they didn't have a show. Yer know – I think they were a little afraid of yer dad – a hard man and not to be trifled with. Oh, yes, the beggers knew what was going on, but couldn't do a thing about it.'

He chuckled and went on. 'I remember a young fella, a whippersnapper, still wet behind the ears, straight from Wellington. He tried to do something about it. They did for him, the poor bugger. Tarred and feathered him, and tossed him into the drink. There was hell to pay. But what could they do about it? Nothing. The men wore masks, and one was clearly a *papa'a* – undoubtedly your old man. No – he was a hell of a guy.'

It's late in the evening, and I'm back in my room, still a little stunned by Miss Black's revelations. I have a headache and feel sick. Perhaps she's right. I may be suffering from sunstroke. But, no – how can that be? I'm Polynesian, and Polynesians don't get sunstroke, do they? I hang irresolutely over the phone, wondering whether I should pick it up and ring Tia, and tell her what I'd learnt about my father. No, I decide. I couldn't possibly discuss it on the radio telephone, what with the static, and the ever present threat of the fiend listening in and wrecking our conversation.

'Why would I do that?' murmured the all too familiar voice of the fiend. He stood shyly on points in the doorway, still in the little pink ballet skirt, head against the door jamb, and looked fondly at me.

'Dear boy, when will you realise I'm the closest buddy you have. If you want to ring your faithful – ha, ha! – wife, why not go ahead before she hops into bed with the leader of the *tere* party now visiting Penrhyn, the man who deprived her of her cherry. At this very moment, she is making sheep's eyes at him, and her sexual juices are running down her thighs.'

When I didn't respond, but got slowly to my feet, fists clenched in fury, and fully prepared to smash that sneering grin on his face, he changed his tune – the coward! – and backed away.

'D-d-d-don't hit me,' he whimpered, putting out a scaly hand, defensively. 'You mustn't take everything I say so seriously. Of course, I know that Tia is madly in love with you, and wouldn't look at another man, even if he is the *tere* party leader. And as for you, old sport, it's true you were tempted when that unhappy dancer called on you late at night – or was it early in the morning? – wearing nothing but a slip, with one tit hanging out. But both you and Tia resisted temptation, and that is admirable and your love for each other is greatly strengthened. Great love like yours is rare indeed, but then you both have had lots of experience. Still, I can't help wondering why Tia stays late, talking to the man long after the others have gone, and even invites him to her home, your own little love nest that you have made together.'

I got so angry I swung a punch, which he easily avoided, dancing away nimbly and pirouetting on the tips of his dancing shoes.

'I've been practising so hard,' he bleated, 'but it's coming, it really is. I'm so happy.' Then he trips over his enormous shoes and falls heavily on the floor, and rolls on to his back.

'I wouldn't laugh, if I were you,' he snarls, the forked tongue flickering angrily.' But I am laughing so much I collapse beside him

'Do you have to wear such huge dancing shoes?' I splutter, laughing.

'I'm glad you brought that up,' says the fiend. 'I so love chatting with you.' He raises both feet in the air, and waggles them. 'I can't help admiring them, they're so beautiful.' He chuckles and turns to me. 'You're a bit of a foot fetishist, as I am. There's something awfully jolly about shoes. A man who collects them can't be all bad. Don't you agree?'

'They're like canoes,' I splutter, still laughing. 'Have you thought of walking on water?'

'If you don't mind,' he mutters nervously, and getting awkwardly on to his feet. 'I'd rather not pursue that line of conversation.'

'OK, then, try this for size. Where's your fat friend?'

Sidewinder laughs nervously. 'You know as well as I do there was no such person.'

I try again. 'Where's Fat Boy?'

'Oh, you mean Inspector Twinkelbaum – he's about his enquiry.' He lowers his voice. 'And I might add, old cock, it doesn't look well for you. But don't worry. Little old me will never be far behind you.'

'Yeah, I know – with a toasting fork in your hands.'

'How unkind you are!' He gives a bitter laugh, then sighs. 'Dear boy, is it all right if I sit down? It's exhausting standing in such large shoes.'

'No, go ahead.'

'You know,' he burbles, tugging nervously at his skirt and giggling girlishly, and giving a little wriggle on his rump, 'I always feel quite at home in your company – almost as if I'm married to you.'

'You are awfully camp tonight,' I remark, frowning sternly.

'That's what I like about you,' he murmurs, giving a little titter. 'Why, you are so firm, so manly. I do so love our little chats. And to think we had harsh words only the other day. But true friendship, like true love needs doubt to give it durability and strength. How can it be true friendship or true love if it's never tested?' He gives a little sob, and he suddenly changes, and I see him watching me with his dead snake's eyes. 'No, she's been put to the test, and found wanting – the little slut. At this very moment, with the children safely out of the way at their granny's what joys, what obscene delights she's tasting with that gross hypocrite, the *tere* party leader.'

I whack him with all my might, and he goes slithering across the floor and crashes against the wall, where he lies winded, and tangled up in his huge shoes, like a drunken kangaroo, or a learner skier who has tripped over his skis and has come a cropper.

'Don't hit me again,' he howls, holding up an arm to protect his face. 'I didn't mean it, I didn't mean it.' Then he begins to blubber, but I'm not taken in. Those cold eyes are watching my every movement, and given the least opportunity the forked tongue will appear and flicker about, as if tasting blood, the jaws will gape, exposing the great fangs dripping with venom.

'What an imagination you have, dear boy – but then you are a great writer – ha, ha!' He struggles to his feet, smiling ingratiatingly.

I have to give it to him, the old bastard! He has great powers of recovery. I watch him closely, every nerve alerted.

'No, no – you've got it wrong,' he babbles. 'You have again tested our friendship, and found that it holds and is stronger than ever. But I didn't like that drunken kangaroo crack.'

'Stronger than ever?' I yell, beside myself with outrage. 'You insult my wife, saying disgusting and untrue things about her, and then you have the bloody cheek to say our friendship is stronger than ever.'

'Untrue!' he yelps back, the forked tongue flickering menacingly. 'How do you know it's untrue? She's hot-blooded and lonely, and her former lover is sex-mad and a notorious stickman, a highly volatile mix, don't you agree?'

I give up. I've simply had it. I think I know why Satan and his followers were chucked out of Heaven. It wasn't so much that they were disobedient and rebellious – they were that, too – but because they kept getting at the Almighty and nagging him, just as Sidewinder has been getting at me and nagging me. It's driving me up the wall. God only knows what it did to God!

Sidewinder suddenly gives an almighty shriek and cries out,

'You know I can't bear that Name, but you keep using it. A fine friend you've turned out to be!' And still wailing, the demon disappears.

I took an hour to recover from the foul fiend's vile insinuations. God how he babbled on about Tia, babbled on, babbled on,

Babylon, Babylonian woes – sickness and corruption. Early shall fly the Babylonian woe. By the waters of Babylon, there we sat down and wept – yea, I weep for you, my darling Tia and for myself. There's no truth in any of the fiend's disgusting claims, I know that, but you are so beautiful I can't see any man in his senses being able to resist you.

Tia, Tia, I've reached my breaking point. I can't hold out any longer. Pray for me. There's a snake in all of us, and given the opportunity it rears its diamond head, and we flop down and worship it. We grovel, how we grovel!

I staggered out into the night, and held my face to the cool trade wind. I drank it in gratefully, and drew it into my soul. I looked at the stars and was immediately comforted. My love, I told myself, is like those fixed unchanging stars. Whatever happens they remain forever true to the laws that govern them. While I looked up, tears running down my cheeks, I had the feeling, the conviction that at this very moment Tia too was looking up at the stars, and having the same thoughts as I.

'I love you, Tia.'

My exultant shout startled a couple canoodling on the dark edge of the pool, under the many-breasted pawpaw. They broke apart, guiltily, as I shouted again:

'I love you, Tia – and shall always love you. Do you hear me?'

And, do you know, I had this certain feeling, that Tia, more than six hundred miles away, did hear me, and that she too was gazing up at the same stars, and was smiling happily, her lovely eyes sparkling with tears.

Cheekily, I called out to the lovers, 'Carry on – seize every moment – good fucking, my friends.'

Then I stood in my doorway, and bowed low, like an actor who had the stars for audience. Then I withdrew into my room, lay on my bed, and slept.

CHAPTER SIX

YOU MAY BE wondering what developments, if any, have taken place in the murder enquiry. As far as I know, very little! Bela's unit has been cordoned off, and the police have spent hours crawling side by side over the surrounding grounds, looking for the elusive clues that might unlock the mystery and lead to the arrest. The murder weapon, probably a knife, hasn't been found, although the long grass in the vacant adjoining lot has been beaten flat by unskilled searchers, who in their eagerness might very well have destroyed the very clues they were looking for.

Shallow rockpools on the reef were probed and rocks turned over, all to little avail. If they had any secrets at all, the scurrying crabs, rudely unhoused by clumsy fingers, weren't about to tell.

Inspector Twinkelbaum has been distant to me, nodding curtly at me if ever we chance to meet – and in the small anxious world as ours has become, such chances are frequent. He is clearly a worried man. He had set his sights on the Kiwi Kid as the leading suspect, and had even obtained a warrant to search the unit he shared with his father, the insurance salesman. The police practically pulled the place apart but found nothing incriminating.

They did find something that greatly amused the investigators. In a small shoe box tucked away in the salesman's drawer were dozens of condoms in a number of different brands. When asked what he wanted them for, he refused to answer – and, quite properly, too. They could in no way have had anything to do with the murder.

But over a beer in the Banana Court Tavern, the town's main waterhole, the Police Sergeant Tai Hoe told me that the Inspector had wondered whether the owner of so many condoms mightn't be some kind of sexual maniac.

'We put a call through to the New Zealand police,' Tai told me, 'explaining the situation, and also to check if he had a police record. The answer came back next day – he was clean, and had no police record. Hadn't even a parking fine against his name.'

'What about his son – the Kiwi Kid?'

Tai laughed. 'The Kiwi Kid! You know the notorious Billy the Kid – he look like him – scrawny, pimply, dirty-looking. No, Wyatt Nuggett, alias the Kiwi Kid, is also clean. He has no police record either. Angels, the pair of them.'

'But why so many condoms?' I saw a young woman at the other side of the tavern, and waved to her, indicating that I would like to speak to her later. I don't know what she made of my signals, but she nodded.

'God knows,' said Tai, his nose in the beer.

'Well,' I said. 'Do you know what I think? Island women, since the days of Cook, Bougainville, and the Bounty Mutiny, have been much maligned and given an unfair reputation for promiscuity. Wouldn't mind betting our salesman came prepared to hurl himself into a sea of women.'

'That's good – a sea of women.' He chuckled. 'Sure would like to see him hurl himself into the sea of our women! They'd eat him up, and spit out the bones.'

'Perhaps,' I suggested, 'he likes to make doubly sure he's safe by wearing two condoms at a time. And, then, of course, he could be one of those sexual athletes one reads about.'

'Sexual athletes!' He laughed. 'Well, I don't think Adam Nuggett would qualify. He looks a weakling.'

'Ah, don't be fooled. As the poet says, a man who passes for bloodless and sexless could be your sexual athlete.'

'Bloodless and sexless,' Tai pondered. 'That describes Adam all right. But a sexual athlete – no way. By the way, you mentioned a poet – '

'Ezra Pound.'

Tai wrote the name down in his police notebook. 'Must read him. And "The sea of women" – is that his, too?' He wrote that

76

down. 'You got yourself a big name in Kiwiland,' he said, putting away his notebook. 'We Penrhyn people, we are proud for you.' He leaned towards me, confidentially, and said, 'I also write po-ems. I take our old chants and make them modern for people to read.' He winked. 'Maybe I become like Ezra Pound one day, and write poems for you to read to other cops like me.'

Is he pulling my leg? I wondered. Then I laughed. 'Sure – why not?' I finished my beer and asked for another, then asked him quite casually, hoping to catch him off guard. 'By the way, Tai, how's the enquiry going?'

Tai frowned. 'Can't tell you much – there's not much to tell. Police work is slow and painstaking. We find little bits of evidence, stick them together, and hope they point to the accused.'

'Do you have an accused?'

Tai looked at me, sternly, 'We got you.'

I almost jumped out of my seat. 'Come off it!'

Tai stared at me until my eyes wavered, then he laughed and punched me on the shoulder. 'No, cousin, you got nothing to worry about yet. You not number one suspect – maybe number three, or five. I don' know.'

'Let me get this straight – kidding aside – am I still a suspect? Yes or no?'

'I tell you straight, cousin. You are number four or six.'

'Stop playing games, Tai. We Penrhyn men, we have got to stick together.'

'Wrong, cousin. I'm a policeman. I stick to the law – to the letter of the law. I uphold it.'

I snorted. 'All right, all right – just don't be a prig, that's all. I'm innocent, you must know I'm innocent.'

'Wrong again, cousin,' he said, steel in his voice. 'I know only what the facts tell me, and the facts they don' tell me enough to be able to tell you yet if you can be eliminated as a suspect.'

'That's quite a mouthful, cuz. OK, I can wait, as long as it's not too long. I have a lot to do. I've got to fly to New Zealand, then back to Penrhyn. Tia wants me back as soon as possible.'

Tai finished his beer and stood up. 'Listen, I don' play games. You a famous Kiwi writer, an important man. You were probably the last person, apart from the killer – ' he paused to let the words sink in – 'to see the victim before she was killed. Don' you see how important you are to the enquiry.'

He has a point there, I thought gloomily. 'And has the Kid been ruled out as a suspect? Naturally, when he did a bunk, I wasn't the only one to assume he was guilty.'

'No – not completely. There are still some questions requiring an answer. But we'll get them. Got to go, cousin. Don' you worry.'

He's no fool, I thought, as I watched him leave. Not as formidable perhaps as the Inspector, but shrewd, nevertheless. But did I see something menacing in his manner, something watchful? I suppose all cops develop it. I had the feeling that he wouldn't be exactly broken-hearted if I did turn out to be the accused. But I could be wrong. Penrhyn people are very close. They tend to close ranks when one of their number is threatened. But Tai, being a senior policeman, would undoubtedly be excused.

I had a good look round the crowded and smoky bar, but I could see none of my old drinking mates. Siegfried was of course dead, and so was the little Aussie used-car salesman, married to a big Mangaian lady who used to beat him up regularly until he cracked and killed her with an axe. And there was the Pommy remittance man, Percival Hardwyke. What became of him, he of the broad female hips and rubbery lips? Accepted back into the bosom of his aristocratic family? I doubt it. No man who falls in love with the Islands ever leaves them. He was a generous man with his malt whisky – a wit, and a lover of modern verse. I remember a drunken evening when he quoted *The Wasteland* by heart – not word perfect but well enough, as far as I remember. I faded away somewhere, in 'The Fire Sermon', I think.

'You wanted to speak to me?' It was the young woman I had signalled to earlier. I didn't know her well, having met her only once when she was performing with a troupe in my motel. She was a hula dancer, a good one, I remember, with rather heavy hips and a dreamy self-absorbed way of smiling as she danced.

'Yes, I do,' I replied. 'Are you on your own? I wouldn't want to tear you away from – '

'It's all right – I'm on my own.' That surprised me rather, because she was a nice-looking girl, if not exactly good-looking. What was she doing in the Banana Court on her own? It wasn't my business, so I didn't ask her.

'I like to be on my own,' she said, sliding on to a bar stool in a very short red dress that exposed her knees and much of her thighs.

I looked at her and smiled. 'You read my mind. Are you often asked that question?'

'Only if I'm here alone.' She smiled, showing her pretty, even teeth.

'Would you like a drink?'

'Just a Coke, please.'

'A Coke, please, Wiri – and a beer.' Wiri was a new barman, a Cook Islander born in New Zealand, but now living in Rarotonga. Not yet fully accepted by his new social group, he was touchy and taciturn, but he did his job well enough.

'Can I ask you why you prefer your own company?'

'You can, but I'm not going to tell you,' she said, rather aggressively, then changed her tone. 'No – to hell with it. I'll tell you – I can tell you're an understanding man. Less trouble, that's all. I can come and go when I like, without having to fight men off.'

'Don't you like men?'

'That's a rather personal question, but I'll be honest. No – not very much. To put it bluntly – I prefer the company of women but there aren't many women of my persuasion in this man's land. So, I drink alone – not too much, but enough to help me sleep at night.'

'You speak well.'

'Thanks – and so do you.'

'Touché. What about your dancing – you used to be so good?

79

You haven't given it away, have you?'

'Given it away? No – I help the girls out when there's a dancer short. They call on good old Naomi.'

'Naomi, that's a pretty name. I used to have a girl friend with that name. She's probably dead now. Two of my old girl friends I know are dead – beautiful girls, they were.'

'Don't cry into your beer, friend.' She put a ten dollar note on the bar. 'Here – have a beer on me, and I'll join you. Thanks, Wiri, and have one yourself.' She looked at me and smiled, and became almost pretty. 'Here's to you,' she said, 'I like you – but don't be getting ideas.'

'Oh, I won't,' I said, raising my glass, wondering where the conversation was heading.

Naomi smiled slyly. 'Tia wouldn't like it.'

'So you know Tia.'

'Of course, I know Tia. She, Bela and me – we were the Gleesome Threesome. Pretty silly really. We were very young. I thought that's why you wanted to talk to me – because of our friendship. That's the only reason I came.'

'I'm glad you came. I like you.'

'All right, we like each other. Shall we dance?'

'Where – here?'

'I was only kidding, you fool.' She was leaning against me, but I wasn't sure if it was intentional or not. The bar was pretty crowded and, as it was nearing closing time, people were beginning to press towards the bar to order the final drinks.

'We're in the way here,' I said. 'Let's go.'

'Tell you what,' she said, brightly, 'walk me home, and I'll answer any question you ask – within reason, of course.'

We stood outside, watching the crowd swirl out of the tavern in a thick cloud of cigarette smoke. Some were clanking with bottles, and nearly all were talking loudly and laughing.

'Well,' said Naomi, 'what's it to be? Are you coming or not?'

'I don't think it's a good idea – do you?' Where had I heard that before?

'I wouldn't have asked you if I didn't think it was.'

I hesitated, feeling quite the fool.

'Look,' she said, squeezing my arm, 'I won't ask you to fuck me, if that's what's worrying you. Men aren't my sexual preference, remember.'

'Oh, all right. Where's the harm in it? But it's getting late.' I tried not to sound cross. I hate being manipulated.

'Poor diddums. Darlingest Mummykins will be so cwoss if diddums stays out late. He so needs his sleepybyes.'

I laughed – the girl was a clown. 'All right, you. I'll walk you home. But no naughty stuff.'

'You better believe it.' She squeezed my arm again, and pressed her head against my shoulder and murmured, 'All right? No naughty stuff. It's not in the contract.'

It's not a good idea, if you wish to remain true to the one you are married or engaged to, to go strolling at night with someone attractive, who is neither one thing nor the other. The air is so warm and seductive, so full of scents that the night seems to release, that it's easy, if one is romantically inclined, to lose one's head, and imagine that one is falling in love. It's a potion that is so insidious that only the most faithful can resist it.

We walked along for a while, saying little, but breathing in the enchantment of the night, with the sea soundlessly gnawing the reef close by, when Naomi broke the spell by slipping her arm through mine, and murmuring, 'I may as well take your arm. You don't mind, do you?'

I squeezed her arm and said, 'Why should I?'

'Good. I knew you wouldn't.'

'I wanted to talk to you about Bela,' I said.

Naomi didn't respond at first, then she sighed and said, 'I thought you might. It's a subject so painful, I can hardly bear to talk about it.'

'But you will talk to me, won't you?'

'Yes,' she said, a catch in her voice. 'I feel I can trust you.' There was another silence, then she said, heartily, 'Well, fire away, old boy.'

'I don't quite know how to put it without sounding crude.' I paused. ' I want to ask questions about her private life.'

'You make it sound grim – but go on.'

'Well, I wondered if she'd had a lot of lovers.'

'You mean did she screw around a lot?'

'Not to put too fine a point on it – yes.'

We passed a hedge of *tiare maori*, and the scent was overpowering. It was very quiet, apart from the sound of our footsteps, and the tinkle of water underneath us, as we passed over a footbridge. As we walked on we passed more and more people out to enjoy the evening.

'Well,' said Naomi, 'in her younger days, she did play fast and loose with men's emotions. It's difficult for a passionate, pleasure-loving woman like Bela not to. Yes, she had numerous lovers – and so did I. Tia perhaps less so.' She paused and looked at me. 'Do you mind me talking about Tia?'

I wasn't happy about this. If Tia had a past I'd rather not know about it. But how could we get a clear picture of Bela, if we left Tia out altogether?

'No,' I said more coldly than I intended, 'go ahead.'

'I hope you don't mind my saying it, but in some ways Tia was the wildest of the three of us. Penrhyn girls tend to be wilder than most Cook Islanders – your mother, for instance, before she married your father, and even later. She had a lot of guts, and was a fighter.'

'How did you know about my mother?'

'Yours was – not so much now, perhaps – a very well known family, and in the Islands the bush telegraph is pretty effective.'

I laughed. 'It's got to be better than the radio telephone.'

'Oh, that – yes, it's pretty hopeless.'

'Yes, dear Tia used to be pretty wild – not that she was promiscuous, you know.'

Thanks very much, I thought. You're doing a pretty good demolition job on her. Aloud I said, 'You didn't like her very much, did you?'

That stopped her in mid-career. 'Well, now that you ask me, I don't suppose I did. But, then, she was always cleverer than me, and a much better dancer.' She stopped and said, 'Do you want me to go on?'

'Not really – but you may as well finish what you started.'

'I don't know what you mean by that,' she said, coldly.

'Well, Tia was no angel, you know. You wouldn't have loved her, as I think you do, if she had been. Did you know she didn't get on well with her father? He was a hard man, and in her unhappiness, Tia had a couple of disastrous affairs, one with a married man. She married the diplomat, a stuffed shirt if ever there was one – and enter the hero, yourself, and you know the rest.'

I was silent for a while, deep in troubled reflection, then I said, 'And Bela was pretty wild, you say?'

'You've seen her dance. Only a truly passionate woman can dance like that.'

'I take it you are talking about the years when she was a girl, a very young woman.'

'Yes – when she was between fifteen and twenty.'

'Fifteen! That's pretty young to be having affairs.'

She snorted. 'Having sex, not having affairs! You must walk about the Islands with your eyes closed. At fifteen a lot of our girls are young women – physically mature.'

I immediately thought of my cleaning girl, who must have been fifteen or sixteen when I first stayed at the motel. She was plump and breasty, and so alive and bursting with animal health that she farted one day as she bent over to make my bed. She covered her mouth with her hand and fled giggling.

We were now walking along a scented lane, giant flamboyant trees arching over us and shutting out the stars. A couple of young girls, walking arm in arm, wished us good night, and then ran off giggling. For such a late hour there seemed to be an unusual number of couples strolling along and talking quietly.

It seemed a good time to ask the leading question, and I did. 'Naomi, do you think one of her lovers could have killed her?'

'You aren't an undercover policeman, are you?' Naomi laughed, nervously. 'I'm sorry. I shouldn't have laughed. It's a serious question, and it deserves a serious answer.' She was silent for several moments, then said, 'I think it's most unlikely, for the obvious reason that it all happened long ago – I mean, the wild parties and the lovers. I doubt if any of them are about.'

'What about the recent lovers?'

'I don't know about them. She has quietened down a lot in recent years, but haven't we all? Can't help you there.' She stopped, thought awhile, and said, 'Wait a minute – there is somebody. Can't think of his name though. I saw them together.'

'Was this recently?'

'Quite recent.'

'Can you remember where you saw them together?'

'In the Banana Court. Bela and I were having a gin and tonic together when a young man, very drunk, weaved his way towards us, and leaned on the table and said to her, "Wassa matter, why don' you come to my place no more?"'

'Was he an Islander, or a *papa'a*?'

'An Islander.'

'What did Bela say? It must have been most unpleasant for her.'

'She said, "Who the hell are you? Fuck off."'

'And did he?'

'Yes – and knocked over a few chairs as he went. He was in tears. It was weird.'

'Did you believe Bela denying she knew him?'

'I didn't know what to believe at the time. But now I don't think I do.'

'Why did she lie then?'

'Perhaps she was ashamed of the relationship. I don't know.'

'Do the cops know about this man?'

'You'd better ask your cousin – the police sergeant.'

'I don't suppose you know his name.'

'You suppose right. But I do know where he's working.'

'Where?'

'At your motel.'

'What does he do?'

'He's the beach bar barman. I saw him there.'

'My god – Tere!'

'That's his name – Tere. He's a boaster, and violent when drunk.'

'Did she tell you that?'

'Not in so many words.'

'But you said earlier she denied having had an affair with him?'

'Did I? I suppose I just put two and two together.'

'Do the police know about him?'

'Ask your cousin. No, don't. Why help the cops?'

'Tell me, Naomi. Do you really think Bela had an affair with Tere?'

'I do now. I think it was a very secret affair, and not surprisingly Bela cooled off him very rapidly. I mean, he's a brute, isn't he? Don't ask me why she ever got involved with him.'

Could that be the motive for the murder? I didn't know what to think. Could Tere be the murderer? He's an uncouth individual, and he only got his job because he's Miss Black's cousin. I had a lot on my mind, and wanted to get back to my room and think about all I'd heard – and I'd heard a lot, much of it confusing and contradictory. But how to get away from Naomi without hurting her feelings?

I was about to tell her I had to get back to the motel, when a large young woman who, I thought, had been following us for some time suddenly loomed up out of the darkness, and cried, in a deep voice, 'I thought I recognised your voice, but I couldn't be sure. It is Naomi, isn't it?'

Naomi didn't respond at first, then said, tentatively, 'Yes – I'm Naomi, but who are you?'

The deep voice seemed to boom in the scented darkness, attracting many glances from passersby. 'I'm Paula. Remember – Dunedin – capping week? We had such fun with you teaching the gang to dance the hula. How amazing to see you!'

I could sense a growing excitement in Naomi and I thought, rather ungallantly, this lets me out.

'I remember now!'

Naomi almost screamed with delight.

Paula moved in, deftly brushing me aside, and took Naomi's arm, and before you could say 'Bob's your uncle', they were walking arm in arm, talking excitedly and laughing.

'Well, now,' said a sneering voice, 'that was a close call. She had you in her clutches, and would have devoured you if her friend hadn't turned up. Consider yourself lucky, my friend.' Yes, it was Sidewinder. He fell into step beside me, threw his arms in the air, and burbled, 'Such a wonderful night for lovers!'

He was wearing his ridiculous clothes, and quite frankly, I didn't want to be seen walking with him. So I said, as fiercely as I could, 'Buzz off, can't you, and leave me alone.'

'No, dear lad – I won't buzz off, as you put it, until you give me what is really mine. You know what it is I'm referring to. But don't let's argue. It's such a lovely night, lovers are walking by, arms linked together. It's true,' he babbled on, 'that we're not lovers, but the next best thing – we are dedicated friends. We work hard at our friendship.'

How embarrassing! People were looking at us, and barely suppressing their laughter. To make things worse, he tried to take my arm, and I resisted as hard as I could, and he almost crushed my arm with steely fingers, murmuring, 'No, don't pull away, my dear.' He gave what he must have thought was a squeal of delight, and burbled, 'You know, my dear, I just feel like a young girl on her first date.' He squeezed my arm and said, 'You know, dear boy, she almost had you – the little minx. She had you almost peeing in her pocket – if you'll excuse the vulgarism.' He let go my arm, tapped me on the head, and said, 'Are you there? Anyone at home? It's hard work talking to you, matey.'

'Get stuffed!' was all I said. Talking only encouraged him, so I was silent and unresponsive.

'You don't really believe that cock and bull story about Tere being the murderer. Only one man committed the murder, and we both know who that man is.'

Then something really chilling happened. A small girl suddenly cried, 'Look at the funny man in the teeny-weeny skirt,' and laughed. Sidewinder's response was terrifying. He turned on her, growling so ferociously and baring his teeth like a dog, that the poor child screamed and fainted. Her father came running up, prepared for trouble, but Sidewinder stopped him dead in his tracks with a glance.

'Friend,' he said, 'the train's next stop is Hell, and you're welcome aboard.'

The man turned away, muttering curses, and no doubt feeling humiliated, as his wife was looking on. 'I'll get you, you bastard, you bloody queer,' and from a safe distance he shook his fist.

'Did you hear that?' muttered Sidewinder, obviously put out. 'He called me a queer.'

'Well,' I said, bitterly. 'You asked for it – getting about in that gear.'

'And I thought you were growing to like it,' he muttered, sadly. Then he cheered up. 'At least you are talking again.'

The incident had attracted a small crowd, and I could see several of the men, talking with lowered voices, and looking angrily at the fiend.

'We'd better be getting out of here,' I said. 'There could be trouble.'

'My second name is trouble,' he growled. The forked tongue had appeared, and I knew that if I didn't get him away, things could turn really nasty.

'Are you coming?' I said, hurrying past the angry men.

'All right, all right,' he said, crossly, as he caught up with me. 'We could have had ourselves a bit of fun back there.'

'But I thought you could only act under commission.' He didn't reply, so I went on. 'You just can't grab anyone merely because he annoys you.'

'Look,' he said in a sulky voice, 'I don't need you to tell me my job.'

'Well, do it properly then. Stick to the rules.'

'How did you get hold of the rule book anyway? It's confidential to the Order of the Dark Angels – or is it the Dark Order of Angels?'

He just never gets it right, I thought. Aloud I said, 'Never mind that. It's not important.'

'Not important!' he yelled. 'You could be an undercover agent as that tiresome girl insinuated. I'll have to enter it in my next report.'

'Do what you like – I'm not interested.' I was tired and cross, but strangely enough not at all scared of him.

'OK, OK,' he muttered, glaring at some night-strollers, who had stopped and were staring curiously at him. He became self-conscious, and started fidgeting with his ballet skirt, and smoothing back his pink candyfloss hair. 'Let's not quarrel. People will think we're lovers having a spat.'

'God forbid,' I almost shouted.

The fiend flinched, and whined, 'Don't do that to me, if you value me as a friend. You know how that Name affects me.'

'Oh, for Christ's sake!'

'There you go again!' He was almost in tears. 'What possible pleasure do you get out of tormenting your old buddy?'

'A great deal actually.' I was grinning from ear to ear. 'Have you any idea how ridiculous you look in that outfit. You don't, do you? Don't they teach you anything in Hell? You have absolutely no dress sense? No wonder people stare.'

Sidewinder was deeply depressed, and hung his head. 'And I thought they were staring at you. I wanted to protect you from their impertinent curiosity.' He was really down in the mouth.

'And you think these pretty things don't suit me at all?'

'I do.' I was merciless. I was getting some of my own back.

The fiend sighed. 'And I do so love pink.'

'Well,' I said, briskly. 'Got to go – cheerio.'

Sidewinder stirred himself. 'Before you do,' he said quietly, 'you ought to know I have a new deal to offer you. No, don't say a word – you can thank me later.' I started to splutter. 'Hear me out, old friend. You'll find it irresistible, I have no doubt.'

'Oh, yeah – like all the other deals that fell through.'

'Not at all – and try not to be cynical. It doesn't become you.'
He took a deep breath. 'Are you prepared for perhaps the most
important decision of your life?'

'Get on with it,' I said, crossly.

'OK,' he said, blandly. 'I know you know that Tere the barman
didn't do it.'

'How would you know that?' Bloody cheek! I thought.

'How do I know?' He was practically crowing. 'Because you,
dear heart, you did it.' And he stood there in the darkness, delighted with himself, as if he'd produced a rabbit out of a hat.
'No, don't kiss my hand. There's a time and place for everything.'

I was indignant. 'I wasn't trying to kiss your hand, you fool. I
was trying to remove it from my shoulder. You have a grip of
steel.'

Sidewinder was delighted. 'That's high praise coming from you.'

'I try to be accommodating,' I muttered sourly.

'Of course you do, of course you do – that's why I value you
so highly. Now, about this deal. Our bovine Inspector Twinkelbaum is about to make an arrest – you needn't look surprised.
You must have been expecting it all along. OK. This is my plan.
Tere will confess to the murder – I'll see that he does. That will
take the heat off you.'

I was shocked. 'How are you going to get Tere to confess?'

'That's a mere detail – leave it to me.'

I was outraged. 'I'll expose you, you devil – see if I don't.'

Sidewinder's jaw dropped, the forked tongue swayed in a kind
of dance, and he chuckled horribly. 'And how do you propose to
do that? No one will believe you. They'll lock you away as a
lunatic – which you are anyway.'

'You wait,' I muttered. 'I'll find a way.' We had reached my
motel, and I knew he wanted to be invited in, but I wasn't having
it.

'Look,' I said, 'I'm tired. You're not coming in – so piss off.'

The fiend exploded. 'I'll see you in prison, then. That cousin of yours, Sergeant Tai Plod, gave you the wrong figures. You're not number three, eight, or any other such number. You, sir, are number one.'

Sidewinder gave a squeal of such concentrated fury that his face turned white-hot and glowed eerily in the darkness. He kicked out viciously at the motel's stray dog that happened to be trotting past at that moment, and thinking that the blast had been levelled at him he howled in terror, and with his tail between his legs he ran off yelping into the trees.

CHAPTER SEVEN

WORSE WAS TO come. Next day I'd barely finished my breakfast when Tia rang me in great distress from Penrhyn. As usual, static made conversation difficult, and I wondered if the fiend was interfering with the sound waves – or whether it was really Tia who was speaking, or some female fiend that Sidewinder had arranged to do me mischief.

'Speak slowly and louder, my darling,' I shouted, as another band of static hit the sound waves.

'I'm so unhappy,' she cried, and even as she spoke it struck me, irrelevantly, that it's difficult to sound unhappy when one shouts. I suppose it's because the lower registers best convey feelings of misery.

'What is it, dear – tell me?'

'I hear you have been seeing Naomi Ruth. Is that true?'

I was stunned – to put it mildly. It seemed but a moment ago that I'd been talking to Naomi in the pub and afterwards on the walk. Whoever the informer was, he or she hadn't wasted any time to put my weights up.

'Yes,' I stammered, 'b-but it wasn't what you think.'

'What wasn't? Do tell me.'

'It was innocent, believe me.'

'That's not what I heard.'

I was outraged. 'Who's been spreading malicious stories about me? Tell me and I'll sort the bugger out.'

'Never mind that,' she wailed. 'Is it true or not?'

'I saw her only in the pub – '

'That's not what I heard.'

'Please let me finish.' Another band of static struck the sound waves, and I couldn't make out Tia's response.

When the static cleared, I heard her say, accusingly, 'Do you deny you took her home?'

'Of course I can. It simply isn't true. I did *not* take her home.' I was so upset I was shouting.

'Don't lie, darling.' Tia was sobbing. 'You have never lied to me before. Please – tell me what's going on?'

'All right, all right,' I shouted. 'I didn't walk Naomi all the way home – only part of it. What harm is there in that? Anyway, tell me who the trouble maker is, and I'll tell you how untrustworthy he is – the bastard!' I was fuming and determined to expose him, and punch his face in.

'Won't you tell me his name?'

'I don't know his name,' she wailed. 'And I didn't recognise his voice.'

Ha, I thought, so it was a man! Then it could have been Mr Trouble himself. Was that a gurgle of laughter I heard rising out of the static.

'And you didn't take her all the way home?' There was relief in her voice.

'And into her bed?' I heard her gasp. 'No, definitely not. It's not like you to be so jealous, darling – so, please tell me what's bugging you – ' Again the all-obliterating static, and I had to repeat the question when it cleared.

'Then you didn't have a date with Naomi in the Banana Court?' There was relief in her voice.

'No, I didn't. I was drinking with Tai Hoe in the Banana Court, when I happened to see her across the bar, and signalled to her I wanted a word.'

'But why Naomi of all people?'

'I suppose I wanted to do a bit of police work of my own. I knew she had been Bela's friend and I wanted to quiz her. You know how curious I am. I'm a dog worrying a bone, when I want answers.'

'Naomi was no friend of Bela,' she snorted, 'or of mine either.'

'I didn't know that. I saw the two of them dance a duet at the Rarotonga a few years ago, and assumed they were good friends.'

'Not true.' There was another burst of static. 'Not true,' she repeated, when it faded.

'And you were never friendly with Naomi?'

'No, I wasn't,' Tia asserted, 'and she never liked me.'

'She says she admires you.'

Again Tia snorted. 'She would say that, but it's not true. She has always been envious of me. I used to get better marks in exams, and I won a scholarship she wanted.'

'But weren't you girls known as the Threesome Gleesome?'

'A what?' Tia's scorn was almost tangible.

'She said the three of you were so close as dancers and such good friends that you called yourselves the Threesome Gleesome.'

Tia laughed. 'Of course, it's not true. It's pure invention. She was always making up silly titles like that.'

'Well,' I admitted, 'she certainly had me fooled.'

'Of course, she did – she's clever.' Tia laughed a little nervously. 'Anyway, darling, I'm glad she didn't seduce you.'

'No, dear, she didn't do that.' I couldn't help wondering what would have happened if Paula hadn't turned up. Naomi was all over me, and I'm not sure – being another weak man – if I could have resisted her if I'd seen her home. Away from Tia, I know I am susceptible to feminine wiles.

There was a particularly loud burst of static, and I'm sure I heard ribald laughter, and Tia heard it, too.

'What was that awful noise?' she asked. 'It sounded like laughter. Is someone playing tricks on us?' She sounded worried.

Someone was, but I couldn't tell her that. 'No, my love – it's just interference from another wave band. It's quite common at this time of year – the so-called hurricane season.'

'Lovely talking to you, darling,' she said. 'I feel much better now. But I wish you'd come home. I hate you being there with all those female maneaters!' I laughed. 'We are all missing you – especially Tieki.'

'But I've been away only three days.'

'It already feels like a lifetime. Do you know when you're flying to New Zealand?'

'No,' I said. 'It's the peak season, and cancellations are rare. But

93

I'm hoping to get one shortly.'

'How do you fill in the time?'

'I work on my novel – but not as much as I'd like to. Most of the time I try to keep up with the murder enquiry.'

'Have they arrested the murderer yet?'

'Not yet.'

'Do they have any suspects?'

'I think they have several.' Where were these questions leading? I wondered. I soon found out.

There was a long pause, then Tia said, tentatively, 'The informer who rang me about you and Naomi told me you were a leading suspect.' There was a catch in her voice. 'But it's not true, is it?'

'The nasty bastard! Of course it's not true!'

'I didn't think it was.' Her voice broke. 'I love you so much, darling.'

'I love you too, darling. Give Tieki a hug from me – and your mother too – if she can bear it.'

Tia laughed. 'I will.'

We exchanged more endearments, and then hung up, just as a huge band of static was about to wipe us out. Tia may not be worried, but I certainly was. Sidewinder was stoking up his campaign, and I could expect very little relief from his machinations. The contest between us would not end until either he carried off my soul, or I had thwarted him and sent him howling back to his master, who, I hope and trust, would mete him out the punishment he deserves.

There was a bellow of rage just then that shook the room. But I wasn't at all intimidated. I enjoy needling him, despite the risk, for he isn't the brightest of demons. His way of coping with a setback or a frontal assault is to roar, and the greater the setbacks the louder he roars. There was another bellow then, but only half-hearted and fading. He has obviously taken my point and will either sulk, or slope off to torture some unfortunate less capable of self-defence. But he'll be back. You can bet on it.

'I will be back. You can bet on it.' He must have heard me, but his voice came from far away. He's definitely on the run. Isn't he?

Tia has left me with a lot of problems. What, for example, am I going to say when I next run into Naomi? It would be pretty silly to cross the street to avoid her? Tia has said some awfully damaging things about her, and knowing Tia as I do, and allowing for her hurt, I believe she was telling the truth. Unless, of course, it wasn't Tia I was talking to, but a female fiend. Which isn't likely. Is it?

The cleaning girl knocked on my door as I was hanging up the telephone, and when I called out, 'Come in – the door isn't locked,' in she breezed, bringing with her the odour of coconut oil which she rubs into her hair.

'Oh, this room is stuffy,' she declared, drawing the curtains and opening the windows.

'You look chipper today,' I said, smiling at her. She has the gift that many Island women have of giving comfort. She is so full of life, so sure that the future will turn out well, that she remains cheerful and optimistic at all times. These are the qualities that make Christianity so attractive to them.

She went out to her trolley and brought in a tray of foodstuffs for my fridge, then asked me, uncertainly, 'Is that good, what you say about me?'

'Sure,' I said, with a laugh. 'It means you look nice.'

'Thank you.' But I could see she didn't feel easy with the compliment, possibly because she was about to be married.

She filled the fridge, then said, 'People are wrong to say you did that awful thing to Bela.'

That was a body blow! I stared at her for a while, while she fidgeted with her hands, then said, sternly, 'What people have been spreading that rumour, Mata? Tell me.'

'The girls in the laundry,' she said, looking close to tears. 'I tell them it's not right to talk like that. You are a good man, and Tia loves you. Tia would not marry a bad man. I tell them you could not kill – you are kind.'

95

'Thank you, Mata. You're a good friend.' She went out smiling, but leaving me deeply troubled. Things are in a bad way, if even the laundry girls are gossiping about me. But who could be spreading such an evil rumour? Not the police, that was certain. Who, then? God knows. Sidewinder's agents? Possibly. It was pointless to talk to the laundry girls and warn them not to repeat the lie. The damage was done. The tiny opening in the dyke was now a gaping hole through which the waters rushed, sweeping the truth away. There was nothing I could do except hope that the killer is caught, and the sooner the better.

I decided to go for a walk to clear my head. Even with the fan turned on to full speed, it remained awfully stuffy. The fan was merely stirring the same porridge, and not replacing it. Heeding Miss Black's advice, I put on a cloth hat, and wandered past the pool patronised as usual by showoffs of both sexes with fine bodies and the skills to show them off to the best advantage.

A superbly built young woman leapt to her feet with a cry, as I walked past, nearly bumping into me, then fled shrieking, pursued by a muscular young man who could have been a bodybuilder, except that bodybuilders pursue other bodybuilders, don't they? There was something rather beautiful in the chase. They could have been recreating the Apollo and Daphne myth, so that when the young man caught up with his Daphne, I half-expected her to elude him by turning into a tree. Some of the bathers glanced at me as I strolled along, but their looks were quizzical, rather than suspicious, and this encouraged me to think that few people took the rumour seriously.

I waded across the reef that the police had already gone over with a fine toothcomb, and I did my own inspection, except that I was looking for sea creatures, rather than the murder weapon. I find it soothes the mind just to peer into rockpools and turn over stones to find what lies under them.

I used a large stick to turn over a heavy rock, and watched as numerous tiny fish darted for shelter like slivers of sunlight, while a big orange crab shadow-boxed warily with its nippers, as it backed out of sight under a ledge. In another much bigger pool, three crabs were dining off a dead fish, its white flesh torn and shredded. Then suddenly I had the feeling that a number of crabs were dining on my flesh at that very moment, and I hurried back to the motel.

The beautiful people were still skylarking at the pool, but a row had developed between them and some angry parents, who accused them of monopolising the pool and not giving their children a chance to bathe. I was amused to see the bodybuilder backing away from a massive Aussie truckdriver, who was being egged on by his wife, a large scraggy woman with a voice like a circular saw.

'Get shot of them wimps and homos, Dave,' she shrieked. 'They bloody well think they own the bloody pool.'

I gave the beautiful Daphne, who was looking on and laughing, a wink, and she rewarded me with a dimpled smile, exposing small perfect teeth. She was wearing one of those togs with cutaway sides and a thin band, encircling the crutch so tightly, it seemed about to split her up the middle. And so back to my room.

I haven't mentioned the happy dream I had last night. I don't remember how it started, and I woke, as one does in dreams, just as some revelation was about to take place. Anyway, I was walking along a leafy lane, perhaps the same lane as Naomi and I had walked along, except that it was sunny and the soft trades were blowing. My companion was a slim young girl wearing a white dress. Her long fine black hair was loose and fell about her shoulders.

We were accompanied by a small crowd of children, smiling and talking quietly among themselves. I had no idea who they were or where we were going, and it didn't seem to matter. Greatly daring, I took the girl's soft hand in mine, and to my delight she squeezed it gently, twice, and left her hand there. I looked at her, and she was smiling.

Who was this woman? I have no doubt it was my Muse. Who else could it have been?

But what was the dream trying to tell me? I searched my mind and could only conclude that my life was about to take a turn for the better. Perhaps I would finish my novel soon and have it accepted by a publisher, and – to crown it all – discover that I could give my darling Tia the baby that she longed for. The happy children surely signalled the happy outcome of my travels.

I don't know what amused Sidewinder so much, for he gave a wild cackle of laughter. But something in the laughter, a sour note hinting so faintly of failure and despair that I thought I might be mistaken, made me think that Sidewinder's confidence was beginning to crack. Could it be that he was no longer confident he would ever possess my soul? But steady, old man, I told myself – don't be too cocky. The fiend has many weapons in his armoury, some of which he hasn't used. Provoke him, and you may regret it. I don't know if he was still around as these thoughts were going through my mind, but if he was he didn't show.

There was a knock on the door. It was the cleaning girl again, come to change my bed linen. She entered the room, smelling strongly of coconut oil and some teasing scent personal to herself. She was clearly out of sorts, because she avoided my glance.

I greeted her and said, 'Mata, I hope there hasn't been any more gossip about me.'

'No,' she answered, blushing. 'Miss Black she told the laundry girls off, and said she would sack them if they gossiped about the guests. She didn't say you, but the girls they knew she meant you.'

I left Mata to make the bed, and tooled down to the Beach Bar where Tere the Atiuan was officiating. Adam Nuggett the insurance salesman and Abe Scone the great American bore were chatting, heads close together, and when they saw me they sprung apart and looked so guilty that I laughed.

Tere leaned across the bar and muttered, 'Don't trust them guys. They hang you if they can.' And aloud: 'What's it to be?'

'My usual,' I sat down on a bar stool and had a good look

98

around at the other drinkers, mostly young people, enjoying a cold beer, made even more enjoyable by the soft trade wind playing on their bronzed bodies and rustling the thatched roof above their heads. It was so gentle that it could barely heave the sea on to the reef, fifty yards away. I became a little homesick for Penrhyn, for the wind was blowing from that quarter, and I had the irrational thought that the breeze that was lifting the hair of the young women seated round the bar, was the same as that which had ruffled Tia's hair not long before.

'What yuh smilin' at, buddy?' It was the boring Yank. 'Wouldna thought you'd much to smile about, eh, Adam?'

'Not much at all,' agreed Nuggett, ducking his head, and looking like a rabbit looking for his hidey hole.

'Watch it,' I warned them both, 'or I'll have you both for slander.'

'Nuts to you, Kiwi!' muttered Scone, dragging his heavy buttocks off the stool. 'Coming, Adam?'

'Go with him, Adam, old son,' I urged. 'I understand you're going home soon. Pity about all those unused condoms in your drawer. Now you'll never get to using them all.' I turned to the others and said, 'Any takers? He has hundreds to spare. See Adam, if you're interested.' But poor Adam wasn't to be drawn. He trailed miserably after the Yank, followed by hoots of laughter. All right, I was childish. So what?

'What a man!' breathed a young woman, across the bar from me. 'All those condoms! You can never tell, can you? He looks such a wimp.'

'No, you can't,' I said, playing along. She was a young divorcee named Bunny, who was fair, rather plain, with bad teeth, and a small compact body, which she kept in good working order through jogging and aerobics. At all times of the day she could be seen tooling along the waterfront, usually alone, but occasionally with some poor stumbling elderly admirer in tow. She'd been making eyes at me since I arrived at the motel, and I suspected that she came down to the beach bar mainly because she knew it was my watering hole.

But I wasn't having any. She wasn't very subtle, having no gifts as a coquette, and it even occurred to me that she might be in Sidewinder's employ, a suspicion reinforced by a dream in which she was giving him private tuition in aerobics. Imagine it. Sidewinder in his ballet dress and enormous shoes, cavorting about like a huge mad hare with ski-like legs. He had no sense of timing whatever, and so he kept tripping over his feet and crashing heavily, each time causing Bunny to shriek with laughter – or was it fury? It was hard to tell, because she would hold her hand over her mouth, as people who have bad teeth tend to do.

But if Bunny was laughing, the pianist certainly wasn't. This was Abe Scone's blue-rinse wife Camilla, who had horsey features and huge hands. I could imagine them closing round her husband's flabby neck and it didn't upset me at all. Anyway, there she was pounding away on her electronic keyboard, never once striking the right note, and each time the fiend fell, she would shriek, 'Get up – it won't do at all.' Then she would pound away once more until the next time he fell when she'd yell the same words. And so on. It was a madhouse.

At one point Camilla got up – and she was immensely tall, well over six feet – and tried to show Sidewinder how to do aerobics, but I could see from the way he backed away, his eyes swivelling in his head like rats desperate to escape, that he was terrified of her. In the end, Camilla Scone lost patience. She picked up her keyboard, strode towards him with every intention of wrapping it round his head when the dream cut out, just as it was coming to the really good part. But, as I said earlier, dreams are like that. Very frustrating.

Bunny was saying something to me. Must concentrate, must concentrate. Where am I? Oh, yes – the beach bar.

'Do you feel like a swim?'

'What me?' I looked at Tere who gave me a wink. 'No, I don't think so, thanks very much.'

'Not here,' Bunny said. 'We could drive to Muri Beach, take a bottle of wine – it's lovely swimming there. I have a rental car.'

'Thank you. I'm not a swimmer.'

She laughed. 'Really? But all Islanders are swimmers, aren't they? Born in the water, and that sort of thing.'

'Give it a go, man,' muttered Tere, as he wiped the bar in front of me. 'Why not? She a nice girl – not pretty, but the body built for pleasure.'

Bunny heard the remark, and pulled a face, and said, 'You make me sound like a car – a sports car.'

'No, sorry – not you, Bunny, but . . . but . . .' mumbled poor Tere, floundering hopelessly. He wasn't dealing with a shark now, but with a much more dangerous creature – an angry woman.

'No, I don't know,' she said, an edge to her voice. 'A body built for pleasure, indeed! Where did you pick that up, for Christ's sake? Not from you, I hope,' she said, frowning at me. 'I hear you're a bit of a writer.'

'Now that I think of it,' I said, joining in the nonsense, 'I might be able to use that phrase – perhaps in my next book. You don't mind, Tere, do you?'

Tere was grinning broadly. 'I give it to you to use in your next book.'

'Oh, wow!' cried Bunny. 'I can't wait to read it. To think I may contribute to a literary masterpiece!' Bunny still sounded cross, but the corners of her mouth were twitching, and I could tell that a smile wasn't very far away.

'Well,' she said, getting up, and speaking in a business-like voice, 'are you coming or not?'

I looked at Tere, who shrugged and said, 'Why not? Muri Beach is a good place for swimming – no sharks, pretty. Go, have fun.'

'You see,' I explained to Bunny, waiting impatiently, and wondering about my relationship with Tere, 'Tere's my adviser. I never do anything without consulting him.'

'Very wise, I'm sure,' she said, sarcastically.

We picked up our towels and swimming togs and were about to get into Bunny's rusty little rental car, when Inspector Twinkelbaum came out of the motel, and called out that he wanted to talk to me.

I turned to Bunny and murmured, 'There you are – clearly our swim isn't meant to be.'

'But he may not keep you,' she said, looking very upset. 'He may just want a word with you.' Bunny sounded upset, but I had the feeling that had been growing alarmingly since we left the beach bar that Bunny would deliver me to Sidewinder at Muru Beach. That was the plan. This was my chance to escape.

'I know the Inspector, Bunny. He wouldn't want to talk with me unless he had something serious to discuss.'

'Tomorrow, then?' There was a snarl in her voice that she couldn't quite conceal.

I shrugged. 'I don't know – probably not. I've been doing little work on my novel lately, and it's beginning to worry me.'

'Your precious little novel!' she sneered. Gone was all pretence of amiability. 'If it ever sees the light!'

I looked at Bunny, and saw in her face a look of such fury I was appalled. Sidewinder himself was glaring at me through her eyes, and although the afternoon was hot I stood there shaking in my shoes.

'Oh, there you are!' Miss Black came out of the motel, and her sheer ordinariness broke the spell. I heard the serpent's menacing hiss. I looked around and to my relief I saw Bunny walking away, dejection in the slump of her shoulders. Sidewinder would no doubt tear strips off her when she reported. In her rage, she lashed out with her foot at the poor mutt that came sniffing up to her.

Miss Black was frowning at me. 'I warned you about too much sun.'

'Thank you, Miss Black.' I was still wobbly on my feet, but I managed to control the tremor in my voice. 'I'm all right. What can I do for you?'

She looked at me very sharply, then said, 'Air New Zealand has a cancellation, and they want to know if you want it.'

'Of course, I want it, but I doubt if the Inspector is ready to let me go.' I watched Bunny enter the motel and asked Miss Black, 'What do you know about Bunny?'

'Bunny?' she said, wondering if I'd lost my senses. 'Who's Bunny, may I ask?'

'She was with me a moment ago, and she passed you on the way to the motel. Surely, you saw her.'

Miss Black wagged her heavy head at me, saying roguishly, 'Now, now, you've had your little bit of fun. You'll let me in on the secret, won't you? What's it about – do tell?'

I didn't appreciate her elephantine sense of humour, so I merely grunted, 'What's *what* about?'

'Your Bunny.'

'She's not my Bunny.'

'Have it your own way.' She turned on her heels, this solid lass, and taking big strides, she soon disappeared into the motel, leaving me to look after her, the familiar claws digging at my vitals.

'I'd like a word with you.' Inspector Twinkelbaum equally solid and imposing met me at the door. 'Miss Black has been kind enough to let us use her room for our little talk.'

He stood by to let me pass, and then followed me into her room. I felt as a condemned man must feel on his way to the block.

Miss Black was tidying her room, and when I entered, she gave me a very strange look, her eyes weirdly magnified by her glasses. Was she trying to tell me something? I wondered. Was that a warning look, and if so what was she warning me about?

She picked up some papers from a small desk, and as she was going she asked the Inspector, 'Can I get you something – a cup of tea perhaps?'

'No thanks, Miss Black. We'll be all right, won't we, sir?' He gave me a look that suggested the opposite as far as I was concerned.

CHAPTER EIGHT

INSPECTOR TWINKELBAUM shifted his massive buttocks on the chair, causing it to creak alarmingly. He grinned and said, 'They don't make chairs strong enough for fellas like us.'

I was trying to read his mind to see if Miss Black's warning – if warning it was – was discernible, and I wasn't in the mood for his ponderous pleasantries.

'What do you want to talk to me about, Inspector?' I grumbled. 'I needn't tell you I should be in New Zealand on important business.'

'Police business,' he said, heavily, 'is important business, especially when it's murder. We won't detain you any longer than is necessary.'

Ah, I thought, that sounds as if I'm in the clear. 'Am I to understand, Inspector,' I said, thinking, by heavens, police diction is catching, 'that I'm no longer a suspect, and you'll soon be letting me go?'

'I didn't mean that at all, sir,' he grunted. 'There are still a number of things to investigate. We may need your help to fill in a number of gaps in our enquiry.'

'What sort of things, Inspector? I've told you all I know.'

'Have you?' He glowered at me, head down, like a bull about to charge. Short greying black curls glistening on his forehead added to the taurine impression. Put a ring in his nose, and you'd have Ferdinand the Bull. 'Think carefully,' he warned, 'and don't beat about the bush. Why didn't you tell us you invited Bela to your room on the night of the murder?'

'Heavens,' I yelped, 'you're not going through all that again?'

'Just answer the question, sir.' He leaned forward, big hands cupped and extended, as if to catch the answer. 'Do you deny you invited Bela to your room after you'd both dined on the evening of the murder?'

How did he find that out, I wondered, my heart beating so agitatedly I could feel it in my throat. I decided to play for time in the hope of eliciting what he was really after. 'I'm not sure I understand the question.'

That really got up his nose. He growled in his throat and said, 'Very well, sir – I'll ask the same question again, phrasing it differently. Why did you invite Bela to your room after dinner on the evening of the murder?'

'Who told you that?' I tried to sound indignant.

'You are wasting my time, God dammit, sir.' He hunched his shoulders and leaned forward even further. A foot or two more, and we'd be touching noses.

'I have a right to know.' I decided to brazen it out.

'You haven't, but I'll tell you all the same.' He eyed me very closely as he spoke. 'It was the manager of this motel, Miss Black. Now what have you got to say to that?'

That stopped me in my tracks. Miss Black was hovering about at the time, and with her keen hearing she could have heard me inviting Bela to my room. There was no point denying it.

'All right then,' I conceded, and shrugged. 'But what of it? Gentlemen do invite ladies to their room – it's not a crime. Yes, I did invite her.' And stick that up your jersey, I might have added.

'For what purpose, sir?' he asked. Was that a faint smile on his face, or a grimace? He was fast becoming the stiffest cop it's been my displeasure to meet.

'For heaven's sake, Inspector,' I babbled, 'you know why blokes invite women to their rooms. Surely I needn't tell you.'

'Just answer the question.' He was immovable.

'Well,' I stammered, 'just to have a chat and a nightcap.'

'Would you mind telling me what you were talking about so urgently that you wanted to continue it in your room.'

What's he getting at now, I wondered, uneasily. 'I never said it was urgent.'

'Couldn't it have waited until the morning?'

My God, I thought, he's beginning to sound like the mother

superior of a convent. 'Yes, it could, but we were enjoying ourselves so much we wanted it to continue. There's nothing wrong in that.'

But back he came like a front row forward going for a try. 'That's not quite true, is it, sir? She turned you down.' Did I detect a sly smile on his face? 'She didn't want to continue the talk in your room. Perhaps she didn't find the talk as enjoyable as you did.'

He's hot on the scent, I thought, but what have I got to worry about? It may look suspicious, but I certainly didn't kill Bela. Nevertheless, for the first time in the interview I began to feel uneasy, and not a little vulnerable.

The Inspector was waiting for my answer, but now he seemed less impatient than before, and I couldn't understand why.

'I suppose,' I muttered, 'Miss Black told you that Bela had turned me down.'

'She did, as a matter of fact,' he said, 'but she told me more than that.'

My heart gave a lurch. 'Oh, what else did she say?'

'She said that Bela was deeply shocked.' He was as still as a cobra that was about to strike. 'What did you say to her that shocked her so much?'

'Nothing.' I almost shouted the word. 'All I can say is that Miss Black is lying. I didn't say anything to Bela that upset her. Merely asked her to my room for a drink, to wrap up a pleasant evening, and she turned me down. It wasn't anything more sinister than that.'

'Well,' the Inspector went on, relentlessly, 'I gathered from what Miss Black said, that you propositioned her, and she turned you down, and you became furious.'

I couldn't get over Miss Black lying. What did she have against me? What harm had I done her? It didn't make sense – unless – it suddenly occurred to me – Sidewinder had been at her, conscripting her to join his cause. No, I thought – utterly absurd!

'Propositioned,' I told him, 'suggests a lot more than I had in mind.'

'Well, sir,' he grunted, 'let me put it to you that you asked her to your room because you wanted to sleep with her.' He eyed me sharply. 'Am I right?'

I didn't reply, because my thoughts were flying in all directions. 'I see I'm right,' he concluded.

What could I say? I did have designs on her, and she turned me down in the nicest possible way, but that was all there was to it. I didn't become furious as Miss Black claimed. But I could see where the questions were leading, and I didn't like it.

The Inspector pressed on. 'Very well – when Bela turned you down you were so angry – '

I protested. 'I wasn't angry, Inspector – but I'm certainly angry now.'

He ignored my outburst, and continued. 'When you left the restaurant, where did you go? Did you escort Bela to her room?'

'No – I went straight to my room.'

'I see.' He digested that for a moment and then said, 'Think carefully. Did you see anyone about on your way to your room?'

'No – no one.'

'Are you sure? No one who might have seemed unexceptional because you expected to see her or him there – staff, for example.'

I thought awhile and then said, 'Wait a minute – I did see someone by the pool. It looked a little like Miss Black, but I couldn't be sure. I thought it was someone on the staff tidying up, and I didn't give it another thought.'

'Are you sure,' said the Inspector dryly, 'that you're not making this up to get back at Miss Black?'

I was outraged. 'I'm not a liar. I tell you I saw someone who looked like Miss Black by the pool.'

'But you're not sure.'

'How can I be? It was quite dark – the pool lights had been turned off. Whoever it was by the pool may have turned them off.'

Inspector Twinkelbaum looked at his watch. 'I have a few more questions. You are in no hurry to go, are you?'

'Of course not,' I said sarcastically. 'I should be in New Zealand now, but I'm in no hurry.'

The Inspector sat up and looked very stern. 'It's in your interests, sir, that I clear up these matters, and the more you cooperate the sooner we'll let you go.'

'Sure – fire away.' I tried to sound casual and bored, but he wasn't deceived.

'I would have expected a gentleman,' he said, sarcastically, 'to see a lady to her room on such a dark night.'

You bastard! I thought, and I stammered. 'Y-y-yes, I s-s-supposed I should have seen her safely to her door, but I didn't think.' I was beginning to feel that if I wasn't careful I'd be in deep trouble.

If he observed my sudden attack of nerves, he didn't comment. 'I may have asked some of these questions before,' he said. 'If I have, forgive me.'

That's big-hearted of you, Inspector, I thought, but I'm watching you closely.

'I'm only trying to get a clear picture of your movements on the night of the murder.' He looked at me as if measuring me for a noose.

'Let me see. You went straight to your room after dinner. What did you do when you got there? Did you read a book, write a letter, work on your novel – what exactly?'

'I read Keats's *Isabella* – it's a poem, you know. I made myself a cup of tea, wrote a few pages of my novel, and then went to bed. As you see, Inspector, a dull uneventful evening.'

The Inspector surprised me. '*Isabella* is about a murder, isn't it?'

'Yes, I suppose it is – and other things.'

'Why did you choose that particular poem?'

'I don't know. Perhaps murder was pretty much on my mind.' I could have bitten off my tongue.

The Inspector was quick to pounce. 'But the murder hadn't been committed then – had it?'

I looked at him and shrugged. There was a certain excitement in his manner that I didn't like. 'Perhaps I should tell you, Inspector, there's a murder in the novel I'm writing.'

He looked disappointed. 'Is that so? I can't wait to read it.' He gathered his thoughts and was again at me. 'Did you have any visitors?'

'I thought I'd made it clear that I had *no* visitors.'

'Are you sure?'

'Quite sure.'

'And you rang no one?'

'I rang no one.'

'Not even Bela – and try to change her mind?'

'Change her mind about what, for God's sake?'

'I would have thought that was obvious.'

'Inspector,' I said, angrily, 'if a woman says no to me, I leave it at that. I wouldn't badger her.'

He gave me a sad little smile, which put me on the alert. 'But she did come to your room later?'

'Yes – she did. I've already told you that.'

'Let's go over it again. She came to your room uninvited – right? She didn't strike me as the sort of woman who would do that. What made her do it?'

I sighed, wearily. 'I don't know, Inspector. I really didn't know her all that well.'

'But well enough to invite her to your room, even though she had turned you down once.'

'I resent that, Inspector.'

'Resent away, resent away.' He was almost gleeful. 'Of course, we'll never know, will we? We have only your word, isn't that so?' I said nothing, so he went on. 'About what time did she come to your room?'

'I didn't look at my watch, but it must have been about four a.m.'

'Why four? Why not three or five? Can't you be more precise?'

'I tell you, I didn't look at my watch.'

'What was the purpose of her visit?'

Police officialese, my God! 'The purpose of her visit? I suppose she was lonely and wanted company. I think she just wanted human comfort.'

'But when you offered her *comfort* before' – he almost leered when he emphasised the word – 'she wanted none of it. What made her change her mind, do you suppose?'

'Frankly, Inspector, I don't know.' I did some hard thinking, and suddenly it struck me that she might have been afraid. She didn't say as much, but she was distraught and tearful. She could have been terrified!

The Inspector said nothing, but his expression told me he knew I was on to something, and he wanted a part of it.

Again he leaned forward and said, firmly, 'I know you have something to tell me. I can see it on your face.'

'Yes, Inspector. I believe that Bela was scared out of her wits.'

He leaned back and smiled grimly. 'Now, we're getting somewhere. But how come it has taken you all this time to reach this conclusion?' He looked at me, pityingly. 'And you a writer, too!' He rubbed his palms slowly, and murmured smugly. 'Yes – that's the clue I was after. I believe she was killed by someone, a jealous lover, who may have threatened to kill her, if she didn't keep away from – who else, but you?'

'*Me!*' I almost jumped out of my chair. But I could tell from his face he wasn't joking.

'Yes – you. This is only a supposition, mind you, but the killer may have thought that Bela was in love with you – why else would she visit you at such an ungodly hour except to declare her love?'

'But I saw her only a couple of times?'

'Yes – but the killer wasn't to know that. He or she may have sensed the strong attraction between the two of you, and warned her of the consequences if she continued to see you. I think the pieces are starting to fall into place.'

The Inspector leaned back in his chair until the rear legs began to complain, when he sat forward again. His demeanour was now quite expansive. If he'd had a box of cigars by him, he would have offered me one. 'I believe,' he said, 'that Bela wanted to accept your invitation to spend the evening with you, but she was afraid. When she got back to her room, she may have found the killer waiting for her. There could have been a row, which frightened her so much she came running to you. When she returned to her room the second time, the killer was waiting for her, and after another row, killed her in a fit of jealous rage.'

I must say I felt so relieved to be in the clear that I almost shouted for joy, but I restrained myself and congratulated the Inspector on a piece of clever sleuthing, and was about to leave the room, when he said, 'There's another matter . . .'

'Oh, no,' I groaned. 'Inspector, you really must let me go about my affairs. I have helped you all I can, and now I've got to get a flight to New Zealand. There's been a cancellation . . .'

'This shouldn't take too much of your time,' he said, reaching for the telephone. He asked the operator to put him through to the Police Station, giving her the required number.

'That you, Tai – Twinkelbaum, here.' And to my annoyance he continued the call in Rarotongan Maori. At one time, Miss Black poked her head in the door, frowned at me, listened to the Inspector talking, until he turned his head, and glared at her, whereupon she withdrew.

'Well, that's settled,' he said, putting down the receiver. 'Tai is bringing round the car, and we're going for a little ride.'

'Do you mind if I ring Air New Zealand?'

'No – go ahead.'

So I rang and was told there had been a cancellation but it had been immediately snapped up, but that I should try again tomorrow morning.

'Thanks very much,' I said, feeling, not for the first time, I was stuck in Rarotonga.

Tai drove us round the coast at high speed, frequently sounding the horn to clear the road ahead of wandering children and stray dogs. As we drove past the airport, the Inspector nudged me on catching sight of a wind sock, and murmured, "'If Jonson's learned sock be on . . .'"

'Where are you taking me, Inspector?' I asked, irritably.

'Be patient,' was all he said. He shared the back with me, while Fred, another cop, sat in front with Tai. The Inspector yawned, clapped a huge hand to his mouth, closed his eyes, and at once fell asleep.

Tai winked at me through the rear vision mirror, and said, 'The boss he often catnaps during a murder enquiry. He works all night, and catnaps in the daytime.'

I was dozing off myself, wishing I was back home with Tia when suddenly Tai slammed on the brakes and we slithered to a halt at an intersection to allow a group of children and mothers with laden kits to cross the road. A small boy was drumming on a tin fence with homemade drumsticks the intricate patterns of hula drumming, watched by his sister, a grubby child, sitting on the ground, thumb in mouth.

'He'll be a great drummer one day,' said Tai, twisting his neck to look at me – or was it at his boss, who now stirred and sat up, rubbing his eyes and yawning hugely.

'You go too fast, Tai,' he grumbled. 'I have the Minister of Transport on to me all the time about your driving. You'll kill an old lady one day and we'll all be in the poop.' He yawned again, then looked at me, shaking his head, and said, 'You've led me a devil of a dance – you know that.'

You can imagine how, in the disordered state of my mind, I would react to any mention of the Devil – I jumped, but at the very moment the car struck a stone, and my head struck the roof.

'Steady now, pardner,' laughed the Inspector. 'We'll let you know when we've finished with you, so you can orbit into space.'

'Where are we going, Inspector?' I wasn't amused. My head was hurting, and I could feel a lump forming.

'Slow down,' roared the Inspector. Tai applied the brakes, and we narrowly missed a decrepit looking horse that had chosen that moment to cross the road.

I regret to say that Islanders on the whole aren't good to animals. They aren't cruel to them; they just don't take sufficient care of them. Most of the dogs are half-wild and underfed. And the horses too look half-starved, and are a sorry sight, with their ribs sticking out, and their coats matted and dirty.

'Bloody hell!' yelled the Inspector, as we swung round the corner and skidded to a stop, with a scene of the most appalling destruction spread out before us – a dead horse, its legs in the air, and still quivering, lay in a widening pool of frothy blood, surrounded by smashed wooden crates, their contents, oranges and pawpaws, scattered over a wide area.

The Inspector leapt out of the car, shouting, 'Tai, get on the blower and ring the ambulance, and, Fred, you come with me. The two of them ran to the truck which was forty yards further on, upended in a ditch. It had literally ploughed its way across an open field, uncovering hundreds of human skulls and bones. As I watched, I was appalled to see their spirits rise quivering into the air, their mouths wide open in distress.

'Shit, what a mess!' yelled Tai, as he ran to join the others. He hadn't mentioned the spirits, so I assumed he couldn't see them. Worse was to come. Sidewinder, still in his ballet skirt, his arms extended in blasphemous imitation of the risen Christ, appeared in their midst, causing so much consternation that they wailed, and immediately disappeared.

'Come and join us, do,' he intoned, and to my horror, he was joined by the other fiends, Fat Boy, Living Doll, Bunny, Belial and Beelzebub, the last two in top hats. All were as insubstantial as the spirits they had displaced. Bunny looked particularly sour, I thought – and hadn't forgiven me.

'OK,' cried Sidewinder to his unholy crew, 'Wait for it – one, two, altogether, *Come and join us, do.*' Their combined voices echoed around the hills. I plugged my ears with my fingers, and to my infinite relief I saw the apparitions fade away, Sidewinder last of all, who gave a mocking little curtsy, fingers girlishly plucking the sides of his skirt.

I was so distracted by these weird happenings, I didn't notice that Tai had returned, until he shouted, picked up a stone and hurled it at a couple of dogs that were lapping the blood.

'You should keep the dogs away,' he growled at me. 'Wassa matter with yuh?'

'Got a headache, that's all. But I'm all right. How's the driver?'

'Dead,' he said, picking up another stone and hurling it at the dogs that were slinking back, bellies to the ground.

'And the passenger, too – a young girl. Christ – blood every-where.' He got back into the car, and I could hear him talking on the car radio.

People had come on foot from all directions, with that hungry look of curiosity that spectators often have at accident scenes. Before long trucks arrived, and soon there was a traffic jam. Then a police car turned up, four cops got out, and got the traf-fic moving again. Then each grabbed a leg of the horse and dragged it off the road.

Suddenly a child cried out, 'Look at all the bones. Mummy, there are dead people here. I frighten.' Then she began to scream. This caused a rush of people to the large churned-up clearing where the bones lay pathetically exposed, and so numer-ous I could only suppose that a massacre had occurred here.

But I was quite wrong. 'No,' said the Inspector, when I aired my view. 'People died like flies during the influenza epidemics, and were buried in mass graves. This is one of them.'

'You mean there were others?'

'Yes.'

'When was this?' I asked him, when he returned after speaking to a couple of ambulance men, who had arrived on the scene.

'About the turn of the century. Hundreds, no thousands died.'

I was appalled. 'But there are no tombstones or anything. Why aren't there any?'

The Inspector shook his head. 'You have me there. May be the survivors were so demoralised by such a great tragedy, they didn't get round to putting them up.'

I shuddered when I thought of Sidewinder towering above the burial site with his evil chums, triumphing over the dead – and me, too, in anticipation. Why, I wondered, had he acted as if the site was his? I thought I knew the answer. The burial site had never been properly sanctified by the church.

The Inspector came back, grumbling. 'Bloody people! They're drawn to accidents like blowflies to rotten meat.' He called out to Tai, 'You and Fred finish up here, and I'll see you later at the station.' He then got into the car and said to me, 'Get in – we have unfinished business.'

'Where to now, Inspector?' I felt I'd been put through the wringer, and wanted only to get back to the motel to work on my novel. I had no worries about Tia. She missed me, but she was a capable woman, and would cope until my return.

The Inspector sat hunched over the wheel, his thoughts far away, and I had to repeat my question.

'Where we were going in the first place,' was his not very helpful answer. He sensed my annoyance, and growled, 'Sorry – haven't been sleeping much, thinking of the murder. It's like a house of cards. You have one card to put in place, and bugger me the whole thing collapses. Know what I mean?'

'I guess so, Inspector.' I had a feeling we were going to drive on forever, round and round this beautiful island. Then it suddenly occurred to me where we were going. 'Muri Beach – that's it, isn't it, Inspector?'

Inspector Twinkelbaum looked at me out of bleary eyes and winked. He yawned hugely and winked. 'We need to keep our wits about us, you and I.'

If he falls asleep, which looks likely, we're both going to die. But I'm a fatalist and said nothing. We sped through Matareva Village, passing a field where boys were playing football, and soon we arrived at Ngatangiia Village where we slowed to a crawl, and finally stopped at the water's edge.

'That's where the body was found,' he murmured, pointing at the mouth of the little harbour that bore the village's name.

'Who, for God's sake? I'm not a mind reader.'

'A friend of yours,' was all he said. 'I can't tell you his name, but I thought you might know. That's why I've brought you here – to identify him.'

'But why do you think I might know him?' I was feeling frayed and frustrated. Damn the fellow!

'Ah,' he said, 'he had in his hip pocket a little collection of your poems.'

I felt absurdly pleased to hear that, but it didn't prove that I knew him. 'I don't know everyone who buys my books.'

'But this one was signed. Do you sign every book you sell?'

'Of course not, Inspector. Can you describe him to me?'

He looked at me and said, 'He's not a pretty sight. Some fish has chewed off his nose.'

'Hank de Soto,' I blurted out. 'The poor bastard. He never had much luck and now he's dead. Well, well.'

The Inspector looked at me with something like admiration in his eyes. 'How do you make that out?'

'A fish hadn't chewed off his nose – a Tahitian whore did. But I won't know for sure until I see the body.'

We drove on slowly until we reached Muri Beach and pulled up by a shed, guarded by a policeman, who came forward and opened the Inspector's door.

'Thanks, Ben,' the Inspector grunted, as he extracted his huge bulk from behind the wheel. 'Everything OK?'

'Sure thing, Boss.'

'Anyone been around – suspicious characters, ghouls?'

'A number of kids, that's all. I chased them away.'

'Good man,' said the Inspector.

Not all, I thought. I could see a couple of black heads hiding under a bush about a hundred feet away.

'We got the body in the shed here,' said the Inspector, opening

116

the door, and was immediately met by the foul stench of death. 'Mind your nose,' he said, recoiling.

I covered my nose with a handkerchief and followed him into the shed, and looked at the body laid out on the floor. It was bloated and naked apart from a pair of torn trousers covering the lower limbs, and was badly scratched and bruised. The face was bloated and pulpy through long immersion in salt water, but it was unmistakably Hank.

The Inspector looked at me, with raised eyebrows, and I nodded, 'Yes, it's Hank, all right – Hank de Soto. Poor bastard – quite chopfallen!'

'Quite what?' growled the Inspector. 'I didn't catch that.'

'It's Hank – no doubt about it. He had a gold-plated nose made by a Chinese jeweller in Tahiti, and was very proud of it. I suppose some fish is sporting it now.'

'You're kidding,' laughed Ben, 'a gold-plated nose!'

'Can we go now, Inspector?' I said, feeling sick. Without waiting for an answer, I rushed out and vomited, just missing a stray dog that was skulking about.

'Get away, you brute,' yelled Ben, aiming a boot at it. Seeing the same heads that I'd seen earlier, he bawled at them to 'get the hell out of it' – but they merely dropped where they were, and continued spying on us.

'Who found the body, Inspector?' I asked.

'A local fisherman. He found it at the mouth of the harbour this morning.'

'How did it get there?'

'Your guess is as good as mine.'

'What about his yacht?'

'What about it?' The Inspector hunched his heavy shoulders and looked sharply at me.

'He was sailing his yacht around the Islands. He wasn't a good sailor, and he was stubborn. Couldn't take advice. He ran his yacht on to the reef at Penrhyn rather than accept advice from the locals. My guess is that he ran into the reef near the mouth of the harbour, but his luck had run out – there was no one to rescue him.'

This is perhaps the place to mention that his yacht was later seen a hundred yards offshore in very deep water, and, as far as I know, it lies there to this day.

'There'll be an autopsy,' said the Inspector, as we drove back to the motel, 'and we want you here for that.'

'For God's sake, Inspector,' I protested, 'do I have to keep reminding you I have to fly to New Zealand?'

'The autopsy is at ten in the morning,' he rumbled on. 'We'll send a police car for you.'

'Can I fly out after that?' I was, metaphorically, on my knees, begging.

'No – we still need you for the murder enquiry.'

'I've told you all I know,' I grumbled.

'Have you?' he muttered, grimly.

'What do you mean by that?' I hate shouting, and here I was raising my voice again – but it had no effect on this stolid fellow.

The Inspector didn't reply, and we drove on in silence back to the motel, where he dropped me off without a word.

Strangely enough there wasn't a soul about, either at the entrance or in the lobby or office. The whole place was deserted, but I had the weird feeling that I wasn't alone, that there were eyes watching my every movement. It was the hottest time of day. Not a leaf stirred in the giant mango tree leaning over the entrance, and surmounted by a tall coconut tree. Then I heard a swishing sound, and looked upwards and caught sight of a coconut hurtling towards me. I stood paralysed – and then something solid struck my knees, and I fell backwards, and lay on the ground, stunned and unable to move.

'Come on, matey,' said a deep voice, 'up on your feet.' It was the big Aussie truckdriver, Dave. A large hand grabbed me by the arm and yanked me to my feet. 'That was a close call,' he said, 'and look what saved your life.'

Lying dead at my feet, its head smashed to pulp, was the motel mutt. I knelt down and tenderly picked him up in my arms.

'Watcha goin' to do with it?' The big man's eyes sparkled with amusement.

'Give him a decent burial – that's the least I can do.'

'Good on you, mate,' he laughed. 'You'll do me.'

I buried the mutt under a *tipeni* tree in full bloom outside my back door, not only out of a sense of gratitude for saving my life, but also out of a need for an ally at my back. If he could save me in life, it's possible, I thought, he could guard me in death. I was beginning to feel I was in no man's land with only three people I could trust: Tere the barman, Mata the cleaning girl, and now Dave the big Aussie truckdriver. Not that I could place implicit trust in all three.

I patted the grave down with the back of the spade, said a prayer, and I was about to go indoors when I happened to hear laughter which I at once recognised as Sidewinder's. It was a nasty jeering sound without any humour in the human sense. I looked round and saw him about thirty yards away strolling in an orange grove, and he was with Miss Black, of all people. They were approaching the gate on to the road, and you could tell they were good chums from the way they were grinning at each other, their heads almost touching.

I thought I would escape detection, but just as I reached for the door handle, Sidewinder looked up and saw me. He said something to Miss Black that wiped the grin off her face, replacing it with a look of such hatred I felt it like a blow on the face.

I hurried indoors, then shut and locked the door, and leaned against it, while I thought about what I'd seen. I must have imagined it! It's just not true that she and Sidewinder are allies. And Sidewinder, what's changed about him? The face was still cold and evil – nothing could change that. Of course – he's ditched his stupid ballet things and is wearing something normal. Well, if you can call a tight black evening dress, pearls, and high-heeled shoes, on a hot tropical afternoon, normal!

He had got rid of his candyfloss hair, and had long black tresses rippling down his back. The only good thing about his new outfit was that he'd find running difficult, and if it came to a race I'd have no trouble eluding him. Small comfort, I suppose, but – who knows? If you keep clutching at straws, you may in time gather enough for a coracle.

I made myself a cup of tea and, as I was drinking it, I thought about the events of the day, and only the dog's brave act gave me any comfort. The rest merely added to my confusion.

Why, for example, did Bunny try to lure me to Muri Beach? Did it have to do with the discovery of poor Hank's body? And how did the shipwreck occur anyway in such fine weather? I kept thinking of the lines in *Lycidas* in which the same question is asked. Milton's friend was drowned when his ship went down in calm seas, and naturally he wondered if the ship had been jinxed. I wondered the same about poor Hank's yacht, but such thinking got me nowhere, and I decided to give it away and have a nap. No sooner had my head touched the pillow than I was asleep.

CHAPTER NINE

IT WAS LATE in the afternoon when I woke up. I didn't feel too well at first. I never do after an encounter with Sidewinder. I felt a dead weight on my chest. I tried to open my eyes, but the lids felt gritty and stuck together, so I took a deep breath and tried again, and this time they parted just enough for me to see I was suspended in that light-green underwater gloom that exists between sleeping and waking.

The electric fan spun slowly above me, churning the air like a separator, thickening it until it clogged my nostrils, making it difficult for me to breathe. On the ceiling immediately above me were my two companions, two white lizards, almost transparently white. Sometimes I address them, and they become quite still and appear to listen, but if I go on too long, and read them a longish poem I am working on, they just drift off to sleep, and remain immobile for hours. It's no wonder reptiles live to a great age. They never hurry if they can help it. They wait for their meals to come to them, and in between meals they just simply take a kip. I think they can teach me a lot. For example, to sit still.

I was slipping back under water when I was jolted awake by the sound of barking. I couldn't work out first where it was coming from – it sounded muffled and far away. Then I realised it was coming from the direction of the back door, and it could only be from the motel mutt I had buried there. It could be warning me of danger, but from what?

Even as I asked myself that question, there came a knocking on the door. What was I to do? Pretend I wasn't there until the knocker went away? But it could be a false alarm. I'd really feel silly if it was only the cleaning girl – but how was I to know? Wearily I swung my legs off the bed, and padded to the door, and opened it. There was no one there. I poked my head out, and felt the hot sun on the back of my neck, and looked about.

There was the usual group of young people at the pool, making the usual racket. The elderly Japanese couple were taking their daily constitutional, and they bowed to me as they passed. Dave the big Aussie truckie tooled along, followed by his gaunt formidable wife, and a flock of chattering kids, carrying towels.

'Hiya, mate,' he called. 'Buried the mutt, yet? Good on yuh.' He laughed. They were on their way to the pool, and I expected another rowdy confrontation should there be resistance there. I saw the elderly German pacing the covered walk connecting the two wings of the motel, a book held up to his eyes. But there was no sign of anyone who might have knocked at my door. I didn't know whether to feel relief or not.

I shut the door and locked it – I was taking no chances. Then I had a cold shower, put on some fresh clothes – grey shorts and pale green shirt – and wandered down to the beach bar where the young people were enjoying a cold drink. There hadn't been a confrontation after all, and it didn't surprise me. Seeing Dave in shorts, his barrel chest covered with hair as thick as a coir mat, his arms like fence posts, they had wisely withdrawn, but not without some loss of face.

'We were going anyway,' muttered the bodybuilder, addressing no one in particular.

'He woulda eaten yuh, Brucie,' grinned a young man, a dark thickset fellow, with an arm round Bruce's girlfriend, the fetching blonde, who was laughing into his face.

I hardly recognised Bruce. Where were the ballooning pectoral muscles, the bulging biceps, the slabs on thighs and shoulders? He had visibly shrunk since I saw him last.

'They not real muscles he had before,' explained Tere, handing me a glass and a stubby. 'He blows 'em up – but they not strong at all. So he loses his muscles, and his friends they laugh at him.'

It's not the only thing he's lost, I thought, looking at the blonde making a fool of herself with the dark young man. Poor Brucie! Was she out to destroy him?

'Any sign of Abe and Adam?' I asked Tere.

'They were in this morning,' he answered. 'But Adam he goes to find his son, who stayed the night with a Raro family, and Abe, he's in big trouble with his wife. She a big strong woman. She threw her keyboard at him and break his leg.'

Tere thought this funny and laughed, but for me it was too close to the dream I had for comfort. I had seen Abe's wife a number of times, but I had avoided being introduced to her. I had heard her playing her electronic keyboard, and it was awful. She had already driven away two families, occupants of adjoining units, and I know that Miss Black had been close to giving her and Abe their marching orders. But with the keyboard smashed and unplayable, Miss Black would probably allow them to stay.

Miss Black – I didn't like to think about her. Her relationship with Sidewinder was downright frightening. What could they have in common? They must be cooking something up – but what? Miss Black, Sidewinder, and Bunny, how did they fit together?

Did Tere, I wondered, know that Bunny was a demon? He had been giving me strange looks, and I couldn't work out why. I had looked at myself in the mirror after I'd showered, and I looked normal. The eyes looked a trifle worried, but then I'd had a lot to be worried about. I didn't look dotty. So why the strange looks if they weren't connected with Bunny? He had seen me go off with her, and as he hadn't clapped eyes on her since then he could be wondering what I'd done with her. He may even suspect – since murder was on everyone's mind – that I'd done her in. So why not tackle him head on, and find out the cause of the strange looks.

So quite casually, I said to him, 'Tere, you haven't seen Bunny about this afternoon, have you?'

Tere, who was wiping the bar, paused for a second, then went on wiping. 'Bunny?' he murmured, and frowned. He thought a while, shook his head, and said, 'Who's Bunny? Is she a guest? Can't help yuh, sorry. Dunno anyone called Bunny.'

Why doesn't he look me in the eye? How can I know if he's telling the truth if he keeps wiping the bloody bar and never looks at me. The nasty scar on his face that he got from fighting a shark had turned dark red, which suggested he was lying, and knew more than he would admit.

'Come off it, Tere,' I said, irritably. 'Of course, you remember her. You told me she was "built for pleasure" – your very words. And she heard you, and wasn't amused. She said she wasn't a car – not even a sports car, or something like that.'

But Tere kept shaking his head, then moved away to serve a Fijian at the far end of the bar. So, in desperation I turned to one of the motel's characters across the bar – a solitary drinker who was always dressed nattily in a yachtie's cap and doubled-breasted blazer, and said to him, 'Now, sir – you were here this morning. You must remember Bunny.'

He wasn't used to being addressed in such a direct manner, so he gave me a startled look and said pompously, 'Are you addressing me, suh?' The whites of his eyes, as I discovered, were like hard-boiled eggs tinted pale yellow. He was not a pretty sight.

'Yeah – I thought you might remember the young woman, named Bunny.'

'Don't know anyone of that name,' he said, testily. 'I only drink here.' And down came the shutters.

So that's it. I felt quite depressed. Bunny, as far as they were concerned, didn't exist, except as a figment of my imagination. There was no such woman they knew of, so I must be loopy. QED. I think everyone in the bar must have heard me make a fool of myself, because all of a sudden there was a gap in the talk, which was only now starting up again.

Tropical storms can be sudden and violent. They can come out of an apparently clear sky, dumping an enormous quantity of rain, then trundle off, leaving swollen streams and eroded hill-sides. Such was the storm that now afflicted us. There was a loud clap of thunder, the sky immediately darkened, and the wind roared in from the sea, shook the tall coconut trees so they swayed giddily, caught the thatched overhang of the beach bar and threatened to tear it off. Then came the rain, falling in such heavy sheets and causing so much steam to rise from the hot ground that visibility was reduced to a dozen yards. Lightning flickered overhead, lighting up the scared faces of the drinkers.

'Let's get the hell out of here,' shouted someone, starting a stampede towards the safety of the motel, and leaving only Tere and me in the beach bar.

Tere calmly went about collecting the glasses and empty stubbies. He said, contemptuously, 'Each time we have storms, the guests they shit themselves and run for cover. This a little storm – nothing – it will go soon. Another stubby?' He made a move towards the fridge.

'No thanks, Tere. That'll do me.' I peered through the murk and out to sea. Huge waves were pounding the reef, hurling sheets of white water into the air. I was about to abandon the beach bar when I saw what I thought was a sail some distance offshore. No – I must be mistaken, I told myself. I strained my eyes. Could I be mistaken? No, there it goes again. I called out, excitedly to Tere, 'Do you see what I see out there?' I pointed in the direction of the sail.

Tere leaned across the bar and followed the line of my finger, and then slowly shook his head, 'I see nothin' out there – just big waves.'

What's the matter with the fellow? 'There,' I shouted again, pointing. 'You can't miss it. It's about fifty yards offshore. It's going to hit the reef. For God's sake, man – we've got to do something!'

'You all right, chief? You pull my leg. No good to cry wolf.'

'I'm not crying wolf,' I bawled, just as a vicious gust shook the bar. 'There's a yacht out there . . . ' I didn't finish the sentence because, for some strange reason, I knew it was Hank's yacht – and that Hank was still on board. How can that be? I hear you saying. Hank's body has been discovered, and his yacht lost somewhere offshore. I'll try to describe the phenomenon, but I'm not sure if I can convince you – or myself for that matter.

Sometimes there occurs a loop in time, when things are repeated. Everyone has experienced a small example of what I mean. I'm referring, of course, to the experience commonly known as *déjà vu*. 'I have been here before,' as the Victorian poet Rossetti wrote in possibly his best poem. The experience has been described as an illusion, and not an actual occurrence. But I believe that in poor Hank's case there was a repetition and that it took place before my very eyes, and apparently – because Tere didn't see it – for my benefit. Which makes me wonder if Sidewinder had had a hand in it. It's the sort of sly trick he would play to unsettle me.

Hold on, do I hear you saying? There wasn't a storm immediately preceding the discovery of Hank's body, so how can something that didn't happen be repeated? A good point, and it deserves a good answer, but I'm not sure if I can give it. It's possible that the storm occurred in Hank's mind, and that it was translated into the physical storm we were experiencing. There was now no sign of the yacht, so I assumed it had gone down somewhere close to the mouth of Ngatangiia Harbour. Naive? Not if you think about it.

'I'm closing the bar,' shouted Tere into my ear. The storm wasn't abating as he said it would, but was in fact increasing in intensity. Even as we stood there, giant fingers took hold of the thatched roof and tore parts off, and rain started lashing us, and as I ran towards my unit I was caught up by a freak gust and flung into the pool. As I thrashed about in the water, I thought I saw Sidewinder's idiotically grinning mug. I certainly provide him with a lot of amusement, I thought bitterly.

'Give you a hand, mate?' Dave the truckie was kneeling on the pool's edge, extending a massive hand towards me. He was also grinning, but I could take it from him. 'Are y'all in one piece?' he shouted, when I stood beside him. The wind was so strong it whipped the words out of one's mouth.

'I think so – I didn't hit anything.'

'Funniest thing I ever saw,' he laughed. 'The bloody wind picked yuh up and tossed yuh in.'

'Thanks, mate,' I shouted back. 'I owe you one.' Another gust almost threw me back into the pool.

'It's a helluva storm, but it'll soon pass.' But even he had to steady himself by hanging on to a rail or a tree, as he made his way round the pool. But he was correct about the storm. It ended as abruptly as it came. The last I heard of it sounded like a thundering head of cattle being driven by a madman into a gap in the hills which immediately closed after them.

It's absurd I know, but my little misadventure made something of a hero of me. The young people thought it was a huge joke which made their day. I think the bodybuilder was grateful to me, because the focus of attention had shifted from him to me, and he could retreat to his unit, and pump up his muscles in peace, and recover some of his confidence.

His blonde girlfriend, who seemed to have drifted back to him, said to me, 'How awful! You could have been killed.' She shook her head, and her blonde hair swung about, releasing its hidden and dizzying scents.

'I know,' I murmured, making the most of the storm.

'But you'll be all right now,' she breathed. 'Can I do anything for you? I'm a trained masseuse. I could give you a thorough massage.'

I must say I was tempted, but I'd had enough of females to keep me going for some time, and, besides, I felt sorry for her boyfriend, who had heard her make her offer, and looked decidedly put out.

'Thanks,' I said, 'but I'll be all right.' But when I got back to my room, a little tipsy from a couple of bottles of white wine I had shared with the stocky young man with whom the blonde girl had briefly flirted at the beach bar, I began to regret not accepting her offer. My back had stiffened up, from my landing awkwardly in the water, and I could have benefited from having her walk barefoot on my spine.

I tried to work on my novel, but Bela's face kept intruding, and I knew I couldn't go much further until her murder was solved. There was a knock on the door, but the mutt hadn't barked so I assumed I was in no danger. I called out, 'Come in,' and in came the stocky young man, a bottle of wine in his hand.

'Is it all right if I come in?' he asked, hesitantly.

'Sure – come in and take a seat.'

'You will have a glass of wine, won't you?' He was a most polite young man.

I reached for the bottle. 'Here give it to me. I'll get the glasses.'

'I thought you'd like to know,' Nigel – that was his name – said, 'that the Nuggett boy was out fishing when the storm struck. He was drowned.'

It's hard to describe my reaction to this piece of news. I hadn't liked the boy, but drowning is a horrible death, and I ought to have felt more pity for him than I did. I have to be honest and confess I was more interested in how his death might affect the murder enquiry. He had been high on the list of suspects, and I had no idea whether he'd been struck off or was still there. It would certainly simplify things should it turn out that he had killed Bela, but I didn't think it likely.

'Nice drop,' I said, raising my glass. 'It's tough on the old man. They were always at each other's throats, but I think there was affection there.' Who am I kidding? I asked myself. They hated each other's guts, if one can judge from the few occasions one saw them together. 'Have they recovered the body?'

'Yes, and the body of the boy he went out with – a Rarotongan boy.' Nigel shook his head, sadly. 'They didn't have a chance, poor sods.'

'You know, of course, he was a suspect,' I said.

'Everyone knew that – but no one believed he was capable of murder, except possibly,' Nigel gave a bleak smile, 'of his old man.'

'Nigel,' I said, 'what are your thoughts on the murder?'

'Well,' he hesitated, 'you must know you were high on the list of suspects.' Thanks very much, I thought. 'I hope you don't mind my telling you this.'

'No – not at all. In fact, I asked for it.' I stopped and thought, what am I saying? 'Do you mean to say that some people actually believed I was the killer?'

'I don't know how to answer that,' Nigel said, quickly. 'You know how it is. Rumours start flying about when something as hideous as a murder is committed. I've seen the Inspector questioning you – we all have. By the way, don't underestimate the man. He's a scholarly fellow from all accounts, and a lover of literature. He's a good friend of Percival Hardwyke, an old friend of yours, I believe.'

'I wondered about the Inspector,' I said, with a laugh. 'He certainly knows his Keats and his Milton.'

'You were number one suspect for a while,' Nigel said, looking shrewdly at me. 'But I never believed you did it.'

'Thanks very much.' I was beginning to like the fellow. 'Would you tell me why you think I didn't do it?'

'It's too obvious, for a start.'

'Surely life's not like a murder mystery.'

'You'd be surprised how like a murder mystery life is.' He laughed, presumably at the disbelieving look on my face.

'Where do I stand in the ratings now?'

'Nowhere on my list,' said Nigel, picking up the bottle. 'Let me fill your glass. You must know you're in the clear.'

'I wish you'd tell the Inspector that,' I told him. 'Why does he insist on keeping me here, when, as you say, I'm in the clear?'

'I imagine there are a few pieces of the puzzle that are outstanding, and he may want you to help him find them.'

'I've given him all the pieces I have,' I grumbled. 'Can't see how I can help him any more. I've got to get to New Zealand. I've been here close on a week, but so much has happened it seems more like a year.' I finished the last of the wine, and yawned, a not too subtle hint that, although he was a hell of a good bloke, it was time he went.

But I wanted to ask him the leading question that was at the back of all our minds. 'Nigel, who do you think killed Bela?'

The bluntness of the question surprised him a little, and he stood with his hand on the doorknob, frowned, and said, 'Frankly, I don't know.'

'Well, you must have a favourite.'

'I suppose I do, but at the risk of sounding stuffy I'm not prepared to say at the moment.' Spoken like a lawyer, cagey, noncommittal.

'You are a lawyer, aren't you?'

'I'm a solicitor, as a matter of fact.'

'Well, Mr Solicitor – would your suspect be a man or a woman?'

He reflected for a moment, then shook his head, and said, 'I can't tell you that either.'

You'll do well in your profession, I thought, as he walked off into the night.

After Nigel left, I wondered if his views in any way reflected the views of the other guests. I rather thought they did because in their company I have never been made to feel comfortable, either by word or deed. I have felt I was under suspicion, the target of unpleasant speculation. I could move among them quite freely, at times invisibly, which is the ideal situation for a writer like me. I observe, but seldom participate, unless to give events a nudge so that they may form more intelligible patterns useful to me in my work.

Nothing much escapes my observation, and if I make a mistake it is generally because of my haste to draw conclusions. Not that I judge, or assume a superior moral position. I'm no better or worse than those I make the focus of my observation. To be a writer I must to some extent identify with all my characters, from the kid playing the hula drum on the corrugated iron fence, to Bela's crazed killer, bloodstained knife in hand. Here endeth the lesson.

Which reminds me – why doesn't Bela's spirit visit me? She could tell me who the murderer is and this would save everybody such a lot of trouble. I could tell the Inspector, who would make

130

the arrest, and give me leave to fly to New Zealand. If she'd rather not be seen covered in blood – she may still be particular about her appearance – she needn't appear at all, but whisper the killer's name in my ear. That's all I ask, and everybody could then go home.

But perhaps the initiative should come from me. It's a risky business summoning up the dead. Not to put too fine a point on it, something could go spectacularly wrong, letting loose undesirable spirits that make life hell for everybody. Summon a spirit and you leave the door wide open for other spooks to enter and torment you. It's a different matter if the spirits themselves make that decision. They then come alone, and when they have finished their business they return quietly to their long home, leaving you perhaps a little shaky, but the sole occupant of your body.

Where then did I go wrong to have Sidewinder on my back? I never summoned him, or any of his unholy crew for that matter, and yet here they are tormenting me and generally making life insupportable. It's such a relief when he tools off and looks elsewhere for his sport, but sooner or later he comes and resumes his puerile sports. As flies to wanton boys – and so on. I ask you, how can you take seriously a fiend that dresses as he does? He's totally lacking in dignity and credibility. How then can I be expected to take him seriously? Don't get me wrong – I don't underestimate him. He's as bad as the next demon, but I suppose I can thank my lucky stars that he's not the brightest or the most evil demon. He has shot himself in the foot so frequently he hasn't got a leg to stand on.

These and other reflections kept me awake despite my tiredness, but I was about to fall sleep when my guardian mutt gave three sleepy and not at all unfriendly barks – bow, bow, bow – which I interpreted as meaning that I was about to be visited by a fairly friendly spirit. But who – I couldn't imagine? So I made myself respectable – tidied my bed, brushed my hair, and rubbed my teeth with my finger.

And there he was, by God! Hank de Soto himself. He was a

mess and he stank like bilge water. He was all skin and bone, scratched and bruised all over, and he had a gaping obscenity of a hole where his nose used to be. He stood diffidently by the door, as if uncertain of his welcome.

'Come in, man,' I said, jovially, 'and sit yourself down.' I surprised myself by not being at all scared of him. He just looked a poor unlucky sailor who'd fallen in the drink. He didn't strike me as at all threatening.

'Are yuh, er, sure you, er, want, er, to see me?' He saw me looking at the gash where his nose used to be, and tried to cover it with his hand. 'Sorry about the, er, missin', er, hardware. I lost it, er, somewhere, in the, er, water when my, er, ship went, er, down. Some derned fish, er, I reckon, is wearin' it now.' He must have heard me saying that to the Inspector, I thought.

'Never mind,' I said, soothingly, 'I don't mind.' Which was a lie. I hadn't seen anything quite as revolting as that gash, which was bluey-green inside, as if gangrene had set in. I tried not to look at it, but all the time he was talking my eyes kept straying back to it, and recoiling in horror. Poor Hank, he noted my disgust, and squirmed in embarrassment.

Hank stayed with me until the first cockcrow, when he suddenly disappeared. I shall never forget the look on his face when his time was up. Sheer terror, as I hope never to see again on anyone's face. But I anticipate. He has a story to tell, and as a transcription with all its 'ers' would make tedious reading, I have decided to tell it straight, occasionally dropping in an 'er' for a bit of colour.

'Well, it's sure nice to see you again, old buddy,' he said, with a sad smile. 'Yuh got it good here, ain't you, though.' He looked about him with haunted eyes. 'Sure is comfy. Not like it is for us poor buggers down below.' He shuddered and lowered his voice. 'I can't tell yuh, 'cause if I do, they're sure to find out and put me in a place a thousand times worse.' He put his hand up to the gash. 'Sure wish I still had that, er, nose piece. Darn draughty without it – if yuh know what I mean.' He tried to inject a little

132

enthusiasm into his voice, but it never lasted more than a second or two, before it flagged. He looked at me and said, 'What you wanna know?'

'It must be more than a year since you left Penrhyn,' I said. 'Where have you been all this time?'

'Would yuh believe it,' he sighed. 'I've bin driftin' about the doggone, er, Pacific!'

'That figures!' I laughed. 'You're not a very good sailor, are you?' I decided to tell him a few home truths. 'And you're stubborn, and if I might say so, bloody pig-headed, too. You don't listen to reason, or take advice. You always know best, and go your own way, even if it lands you in the shit, and you never learn from your mistakes. What have you got to say to that?'

I could see I had hurt Hank's feelings, because he sat there, head bowed, his breath bubbling disgustingly in what used to be his nose. 'Put like that,' he mumbled, 'I don' come out of, er, it too good, do I?'

'No, you don't,' I said, continuing to lay it on, 'you're a disaster. You ran on to the reef in Penrhyn, because you thought you knew better than the locals how to navigate the channel, even though you'd never been there before, and, inevitably, you got into trouble, and had to call on them for their help.'

Hank raised his head and looked at me, his eyes dull with self-pity. 'I never did get it right, did I? Not once I didn't.' And he shook his head, bemused by the injustice of his lot.

Oh, Lord, I thought, he's going to cry on my shoulder. Aloud I said, 'Have you ever done anything in your life that you're proud of?'

'Now, yuh been sarcastic.' He sat there, head bowed, a hand on each knee, very much the neglected small boy, sniffing back his tears.

'You drifted round for a year, did you say?'

'I didn't say – but OK it was about a year.'

'What – just drifting round?'

'Yeah, that's about it – just driftin' round and round in a bloody ocean current. Yuh wouldn' read about it.'

'I don't understand.'

'Listen – a whale busted m' rudder. OK? Came up underneath big as a hill, and snapped it, er, off. It was the darndest thung.'

'What did you do?' I didn't know whether to believe him.

'Wal, I hung in there. Only thing I could do. Thought the boat would capsize, it shipped a lot of water, but righted itself. Sure was a dandy little craft.'

'But you had an engine – couldn't you have driven out of your difficulty?'

Hank laughed. 'It's easy, er, to see you ain't been a sailor. Why you'd go roun' and roun', and end up yer own asshole – if you'll pardon the expression.'

'It's good to see you laughing, Hank,' I said, laughing with him. 'Things can't be too bad.'

He snorted. 'Are yuh kiddin'? Things couldn' be worse. I'm dead, dead, dead. I'm a young man, fer Chris' sake, and I'm fuckin' dead. And don' say we all haf ter die one day, and all that crap. I got plenty to be sorry about, I tell yuh.'

'All right, all right, Hank,' I said, soothingly. 'I didn't mean to upset you.'

'Course you didn', old buddy,' he said, dejectedly, 'but you know how it is. Ain't got much to celebrate, have I?'

I didn't know what to say. His self-pity was fat as a porker. I wasn't inclined to feed it. I looked at Hank so sunk in despair he looked like one of the damned in the Sistine Chapel. He was beginning to slip away, and if I didn't watch out he'd disappear before I found out all I needed to know.

'How are you, Hank?' I asked, gently.

'Not so good, old buddy,' he whispered. 'Not so good.' He shook his head, despairingly. 'Guess, I'll have to slip back before they miss me – or they'll send the hounds after me.'

'Wait,' I said, stretching out a hand, 'there are a few questions I still want to ask you.'

Hank looked at me, and said, weakly, 'Fire away, old buddy.'

'OK – thanks, Hank.' It was extraordinary. His outline was

beginning to blur. I'd have to hurry. 'This is what puzzles me. For a week up to the time your body was found, the weather had been fine, and yet your yacht apparently struck a reef near Ngatangiia and sank. How do you explain that?'

Hank took a deep breath and sighed, 'It's like this. The whale had made quite a big hole in the stern bigger 'n' I realised. I stuffed an old sail into it, and that kept the water out for a while, but not fer long. Nothin' I could do about it. After weeks of driftin', er, around, the hole got bigger 'n' bigger, and the yacht developed a list – the stern went down, and the, er, bow up.'

'But didn't you run across any vessel that might have helped you?'

'You know, I can't unnerstand it. In all the months I drifted, er, about not one bloody ship did I see.' He shook his head. 'Felt I was in some kind of time warp – if yuh know what I mean?'

'Drifting about all that time, you must have run out of food.'

'Sure did.' He scratched his chin. 'Got by at first on flyin' fish. Had an old, er, kerosene lamp that I lit up at night, and put on deck. The fish'd be attracted by the light and fly aboard. I had more 'n' enough to eat until one hit the lamp and knocked the damn thing overboard.'

'How did you get on for water?'

'Wal, in time the tank ran dry. So I strung a plastic sheet across the, er, deck, and caught what rain there was. Then there was no more rain, and I got so thirsty I drank, er, sea water.'

'That was a pretty dumb thing to do.'

He wasn't at all put out. 'Sure it was – but I got kinda crazy, and I didn' know what I was doin'.' He looked at me and said, 'Have you ever bin so thirsty you went clean off your, er, rocker?' I shook my head. 'No – thought not,' he said, rather smugly. 'That's what happened to yours truly. It was like a storm in my head – if yuh know what I mean – raging for God knows how long.'

So, my speculations in the beach bar were right after all! It had been fine and the seas calm, but there was a storm every bit as violent in poor Hank's mind – a mental storm. I was quite excited at the confirmation of what must have seemed a wacky theory.

Hank was going dimmer by the minute, and I knew that at any time now he'd disappear altogether.

'So, is this what happened?' I asked quickly. 'Your boat was driven on to rocks, and you were flung on to the reef by the impact?'

Hank smiled faintly. 'Impact? There was no impact. She'd finally filled up with water and, er, sank 'bout fifty yards offshore. You could say she made landfall – just.'

I was puzzled. 'If you weren't thrown on to the reef – how did you get there?'

'You won't believe this, old son, but the last thing I remember was being pushed along by a coupla dolphins.'

'And you died, you think, before they had pushed you ashore?'

'I'd say so – yeah, sure.' He looked down at himself, and smiled bleakly. 'The batteries are runnin' flat – gotta go now.'

'Wait,' I cried, 'I need help.'

'Don't we all,' he murmured, sadly.

'Can't you tell me who killed Bela? Got to find out, or I'll never leave the island.'

'Bela?' He shook his head. 'Can't say I know the lady. No can't help you there, old son.' And just as he was disappearing, he warned me, 'Watch out for Sidewinder – if you value your soul.'

'I will – and thanks. By the way, any message I could give your folk?' I meant well, but he greeted the offer with ironic laughter as thin as a grasshopper's fart. And I was alone once more.

You know, I think old Sidewinder is scared of the mutt. I was woken up in the night by the sound of furious barking, and the voice of the fiend bellowing, 'Get down, you brute. Damn and blast – leggo my leg. Ouch! Bloody hell – leggo my hand . . . '

I went to sleep, I'm sure, with a smile on my face.

CHAPTER TEN

I WAS VERY woozy when I woke up, but at least I had slept soundly – I think. It may seem odd, but my talk with Hank lifted my spirits a little. What I fear most is the irrational. I don't object to things that can't be explained. There are plenty of such things lying about in my mind, like bits of meteorites from outside my skull. I let them be, shoving them aside with my foot only if they are lying where someone might trip over them. They mean nothing to me. I don't see them as a threat at all. No, what I think of as irrational is something that doesn't make sense whatever angle you view it from. This is what I find threatening – this is what Sidewinder represents.

You might think Hank's behaviour was irrational. But was it? Not if he had been aware of what he was doing, even if the outcome was not only unexpected, but disastrous. He would have acted irrationally if he'd known that a particular course of action would turn out badly, but went ahead with it all the same. Hank never doubted that he knew as well as the local fishermen how to navigate the channels of Penrhyn. He had the sublime confidence of a fool. Nothing dented it, not even running on to a reef at Taruia Passage. The reef was at fault. It shouldn't have been there.

I had breakfast in my room – cereals and milk, pawpaw, and a gala apple. I'm a light feeder. I decided to spend the morning on my novel. I had made little progress on it lately, and I was getting worried. Not that I ever suffer from writer's block. My main problem is the opposite to that. The stuff pours out of me in such volume that I find I can't keep up, so that good ideas are sometimes lost. Perhaps if I had a secretary I wouldn't have that problem. Or maybe the presence of one might inhibit the flow, and cause me to dry up. I don't know.

Well, there I was, ballpoint in hand, a blank white sheet before me, when I thought I heard a dog whimpering. I was still a little dopey and couldn't work out at first where it was coming from. Then, of course, it struck me. It was coming from the direction of the back door. Was it an injured dog that needed my attention? I sighed, and laid down my pen, and went and opened the door, and what I saw horrified me. The grave in which I'd buried the mutt had been dug up and the earth scattered about the edge. Bits of the animal had been torn off, as if during a fight – part of an ear, small pieces of skin and hair and a large piece, and, inexplicably, the scrotum. The rest of the dog lay partly buried, feet uppermost. It looked as if some large animal had dug it up with its paws, and tried to pull it out, but had been disturbed.

I was completely baffled. What animal had done this? It's true, as I mentioned earlier, many of the Island's dogs are undernourished. But would they dig up a dog's corpse to eat it? There's a saying that dog eats dog, but is it true that dogs are cannibals? In the extremities of starvation, I thought they could be, but perhaps not otherwise.

While these questions were buzzing around inside my head, I saw something a few feet away from the grave. It was a small piece of some black material. I picked it up and examined it, and found it was velvet cloth. From its rough edges, I deduced it had been torn off a dress. Further away were other pieces of velvet, all of them small except one quite large piece. I was puzzling over this, when something made me look in the mutt's mouth. I got the spade and gently removed the earth from around it, and saw what I was afraid to see – a number of black threads caught in the teeth!

I knew at once what had happened. Sidewinder had come sneaking round the back door, hoping to catch me asleep, or surprise me with my back turned. He had disturbed the mutt, who tried to warn me. A fierce struggle had then followed, with the mutt tearing pieces off Sidewinder's velvet dress, and suffering a number of injuries in the process. Who had won? There was no

way of knowing, but from the signs lying about me it was probably a draw.

I heard the mutt whimper again, and it seemed to be coming
from the pawpaw tree that leaned over the back door. It sounds
unbelievable, I know, but I was sure it came from the mutt's
spirit that was perched somewhere in the branches, and although I was thoroughly confused and sickened by what I had
seen, I immediately thought of Marvell's lines, 'There like a
bird it sits, and sings / Then whets, and combs its silver wings.'
The thought of the mutt's spirit perched there like a bird at first
struck me as funny, until I thought of the terror he must have
felt when the demon attacked him, and I wanted him to know
that I would always be grateful to him, and that no matter what
happened I would remember him as a true friend. But like any
other poor forked creature I am cursed with self-consciousness,
and even as I was standing there, addressing the mutt's spirit, I
was all the time conscious that someone, perhaps the cleaning
girl, could come round the corner, and catch me apparently
talking to a tree – like the Prince of Wales.

There came the whimper again, and I was embarrassed to
discover that the spirit was in another part of the tree, and
nowhere near the spot I was addressing. If the mutt had a sense
of humour, I thought, he must surely be amused. I think I lo-
cated the exact spot where he was perched, for the next time he
whimpered he was only an arm's length away. Even if he'd been
visible, he wouldn't have been easy to see because of the dense
branches and clustered fruit.

But why was he whimpering? Was he hurt? I had a packet of
Band-aids in my travel bag, but how do you bind up a spirit's
injury? No, he must be wanting something else. Did he want
his body decently buried? That must be it, for he made a sound
that struck me as acquiescent. I covered his poor torn body,
with the deference to a fellow creature who had, inexplicably,
chosen to be my ally and guardian. Then I patted the soil down
with the spade, placed on it some sprigs of *tiare maori*, the

sweet-scented wild gardenia, and then returned to my room.

Again I sat, my pen poised above the paper, when another knock came. 'Come in,' I shouted, and in hurried the cleaning girl, with my change of bed linen. God, I thought – will I never be allowed to get on with my writing!

'Oh,' she exclaimed, as she stripped down the bed, 'everybody's talkin' about the dog-fight last night behind your unit.'

That gave me a shock. Why didn't I hear it? I pretended not to know what she was talking about. 'A dog-fight outside my unit – what do you mean?'

'Didn't you hear it? People say it was a horrible noise.' She was an efficient worker, with swift decisive movements. She made the bed in a matter of minutes. 'Everyone was talking about it in the restaurant this morning.'

I thought of lying, saying that I had heard it, but where would that take me? So I admitted I hadn't heard it.

'My,' she said, giving me an amused look, 'you must be a heavy sleeper! My dad, he's a heavy sleeper. He goes to the Banana Court and drinks till closing time, then comes home and sleeps. My mum gets so wild she shouts at him. But it does no good. He still goes and gets drunk.'

She is a naive young woman, so I didn't take offence. She wouldn't recognise an innuendo if she tripped over one.

'I'm usually a light sleeper,' I told her. 'But I was exhausted last night and slept right through.' But why, I wondered, didn't the fight waken me, if it had been as loud as the girl said it was? I tried to get on with my writing, after she had gone, but the question wouldn't go away, so I threw my pen down and went for a walk. I thought I'd have a stubby at the beach bar, forgetting it had been damaged in the storm.

A shelf of spirits had collapsed, and Tere was cleaning up the mess. 'Wouldn't you know it!' he grumbled. 'The best whisky, Johnny Walker Black Label – *kaput*.'

'Well,' I said, 'I'm not a whisky drinker any more, so I won't shed any tears. What I'd like is a nice cold stubby, my usual brand.'

'Bar closed, chief – try the bar inside.'

The storm had cleared the air, so that it sparkled, and the trade wind, softer and more caressing than before, was blowing in from the sea. The trade winds – they epitomise the tropics for me. Add to them the warmth and kindness of the people and the curious mix of modesty and frank sexuality of the women, and you can realise how easy it was for the *papa'a* – including my father – to go native.

'Why the scrotum?' I must have spoke the words aloud, because a young couple walking arm in arm along the beach towards me, looked at me and then at each other in astonishment, and then laughed. I looked back at them, and saw they were looking back at me, still laughing. I was tempted to test the Japanese couple, who were the next to pass me, by saying 'Good scrotum' to them. If they weren't proficient in English, they might think it was a form of greeting. I resisted this childish impulse, which was just as well, because I discovered later that the gentleman, a distinguished professor of medicine in his own country, spoke perfect English.

All right, then: why the scrotum? This query was a delayed reaction to what I had found on the mutt's grave. Why did the fiend tear off this particular piece of its anatomy? Was it accidental, or was it deliberate? I had no doubt whatsoever it was the latter. Nothing that the fiend did was ever accidental, even though, through incompetence he botched up nearly everything he did. No, the fiend knew I would find it and construe it as he intended me to. In his nasty way, he was drawing attention to my sterility, and making a mock of it. I don't think I have ever hated Sidewinder as much as I did then.

The thought that now ran through my mind was hardly a noble one. Now that the mutt has been mutilated, would he be able to warn me of danger? I gave a lot of thought to this question and concluded that it wouldn't, because it would be the mutt's spirit that would come to my aid, and not his physical body, which was dead anyway.

As I was cutting across a clearing, heading for the main road, I had the feeling that I was experiencing a false peace, and that at any time now I'd have a deadly fight on my hands. A sense of doom hung over me, and as I looked about me the words of a gentle poet came to mind: 'Look thy last on all things lovely/ Every hour'. Every house I passed, no matter how squalid and tumbled-down, squatted on a well-trimmed lawn, surrounded by coconut trees, flowering and sweet-scented shrubs, some orange and banana trees, its paths vividly defined by crotons – the lot enclosed by hibiscus hedges forever, it seemed to me, in flower.

Giant flamboyants lined the road, their branches interlocking overhead to form an immense cathedral avenue along which sped the tearaway citizens of this beautiful island, some of whom regularly add their blood to the royal purple with which the great trees stain the road. Wild bananas grew along the roadside, dangling their purple horse pizzles alongside bunches of green fruit, and here and there were wild pawpaws hung with many breasts like the Earth Mother herself.

Back at the motel I got a reception I could have done without. Miss Black lumbered out of her office, her square jaw set pugnaciously. I was about to pass her when she growled, 'The Inspector wants to see you.' Her eyes, hugely magnified by her lenses, were wild. I remember seeing the eyes of horses spooked by lightning – hers looked exactly the same! Was she going nuts?

'The Inspector – what does he want?' I groaned. Not another session surely! 'Where can I find him?'

'He's waiting for you in your unit.' She grinned and licked her lips.

I was outraged. 'What's he doing there?'

'Oh, don't worry,' she smirked. 'He's got a search warrant.'

'What the hell for?'

'You'll find out.' And she whipped back into her office, which astonished me for such a big woman.

I was so furious I could hardly wait to tear a piece off the Inspector. I found him sitting in my chair, my copy of Keats in his hand. Tai Hoe was sitting by the window, picking his teeth.

'I'm not pleased to see you, Inspector,' I said, angrily. 'You've no right to be in my room.'

'I have every right,' he said, calmly. 'I have a search warrant.' He passed it to me, but I knocked it out of his hand. He reached down, picked it up, and passed it to me again.

'I don't want to see the bloody thing,' I grumbled. 'I'll take your word for it.' I looked at the book in his hands, and said sarcastically, 'I'm glad that Keats is helping you in your enquiry.'

He put the book down and sighed. 'If you'll calm down, sir, I'll tell you why we're here.' He gave me a long searching look that made me squirm.

'We got an anonymous call at the station that we would find an object in your room that would assist us in our enquiry.' A poetry lover, I thought, and he uses police officialese! He must have seen the sneer on my face, because he stopped and looked at me, then went on. 'We gave your room a thorough search, and at first found nothing. Then Tai here happened to look up at the fan and went away and fetched a ladder, and found this taped to the top side of one of the blades.' The Inspector produced a large manila envelope from which he drew a long-bladed carving knife, and held it towards me, and asked, 'Do you recognise this?' He turned it over in his hands.

'No – absolutely not!' I was so shocked I could only stare at the knife.

'Are you sure?' There was menace in his voice that knocked the props from under me.

I gulped, took a deep breath and tried to control the tremor in my voice. 'Of course I'm sure. I have never seen that knife before, and I have absolutely no idea how it got there.'

'Do you think,' he asked, a glint in his eyes, 'that someone is trying to frame you?'

Before I could reply Tai gave a snort, but whether at me or the

Inspector, I had no idea. The Inspector gave him a warning look, and turned back to me, repeating his question.

'Well,' I said, without conviction, 'it looks that way, doesn't it?'

He smiled thinly and said to Tai, 'Does it look that way to you, Sergeant?' Tai shrugged and said, 'If you want my opinion – '

'I don't want your opinion, Tai – just answer the question.'

'OK, then – well, yes. I do think someone is trying to frame him.'

'Oh, you do, do you?' said the Inspector. 'It's well known how you Penrhyn people stick together. What gives you special insights denied to us lesser mortals?' He got heavily to his feet, and seeing Tai scowling angrily, he said, 'Relax, Sergeant – I agree with you. I think the knife was planted there.'

These were the sweetest words I'd heard in a long time. I'd been let off the hook. But who'd do such a thing?

The Inspector answered my question. 'You have a bad enemy – a pretty nasty one.'

'Do you think the killer put it there?' I said, still shaken by the hoops he had put me through.

'Not necessarily,' he said. 'It could have been someone who hates your guts and wanted to see you suffer.'

'Well, he certainly did that,' I said, adding quickly, 'It was a man, wasn't it Inspector?'

'We aren't sure,' he replied. 'Whoever it was spoke in a disguised voice.'

'It was a deep voice,' said Tai, who, I learnt later, had answered the call.

'Yes – but it could have been a woman muffling her voice and speaking low.'

I knew at once who it was, but I wasn't going to voice my suspicion to the Inspector. There was no need to, was the expression I read on his face. He knew as well as I who was responsible.

'It's a kitchen knife,' he said, turning it over in his hands, 'with a broad blade, as you can see. Bela was killed by a knife with a narrow blade, almost a stiletto. Well,' he murmured, 'there's one thing we've learnt, and that is the person who planted this knife couldn't have been the murderer – unless he or she is playing a very subtle game.'

The Inspector got to his feet and gave me a friendly glance. 'How's the novel going?'

'Not very well,' I grumbled. 'I keep getting interrupted.'

'It's all grist to the mill,' he laughed. 'Come along, Sergeant. We have a few questions to put to Miss Black.'

'Do you want me to accompany you?' I asked, tentatively.

'Whatever for?' the Inspector said, and added, 'No, get on with your novel. Tai and I can't wait to read it.' And with that gratuitous backhander the pair left the room, both chuckling over my discomfort.

I was glad to be left alone, for I had much to think about. I think I had suspected Miss Black from the beginning, ever since I had recognised her as tidying the pool the night before the murder. The pool is close to Bela's unit, so Miss Black's presence there struck me, and possibly the Inspector, too, as highly suspicious. But now, by her spiteful act in planting the knife, she had eliminated herself as a murder suspect. She had been the strongest suspect, now the field was wide open again.

Tia chose this moment to ring me, and hearing her dear voice made me realise how much I was missing her. 'Hello, darling, how are you? I miss you so much. I hoped you'd be back home by now. How much longer will you be detained in Rarotonga?'

'Not much longer, I hope,' I said. 'I think the murder is close to being solved.' There was little static, so I assumed the storm had cleared the air. Sidewinder, too, must be having an off-day. He was probably tormenting some other poor bastard.

'Can you hear me, darling?' Tia has a lovely voice, pure and sweet. 'I haven't been well.'

Tia not well! I suddenly had a sinking feeling in my stomach, and couldn't speak for a while.

'Are you there, my darling?'

'Yes, I'm here,' I said, adding quickly, 'Look, I'm calling off my trip to New Zealand, and coming home.'

'Don't do that,' she said. 'It's nothing to worry about. I think I'm a little run down, that's all. The visit of the *tere* party took it out of me. They flew out this morning, thank God!'

'Are you sure?' Tia had never been sick before in my experience, and I couldn't help feeling this was something quite serious.

'Yes, I'm sure.' She laughed, but rather nervously, I thought. 'I shouldn't have mentioned it.' Then she spoke off-phone, 'As soon as I've spoken to Papa, you can have a word with him, but not before.' Then she returned to me. 'Sorry about that, dear. Tieki wants a word with you. I'll put him on soon. What were we saying?'

'I told you I wanted to come straight home, but you told me not to worry, because it isn't serious. I don't know what to do.'

'I won't hear of you coming back until you've seen a specialist,' she said, firmly. 'I shouldn't have told you I wasn't well – it was selfish, and I'm sorry. You have nothing to worry about here. Mama is well and is asking after you. And the twins miss you. Heavens, I'm speaking as if you've been ages away!'

'It feels like ages, my darling,' I said. 'It shouldn't be long now, before the Inspector lets me go. So, any day now I'll be off to Kiwiland.'

'Thank God for that! It must have been awful for you being a suspect. It's so absurd. How can anyone suspect you of anything so horrible.'

'Well,' I assured her, 'it's almost over.'

'Goodbye, darling – I'll let you go now. I love you.' Her voice sounded shaky, and I couldn't help wondering if she was in tears. Or was it the effect of the air waves? I hoped it was the latter. 'Tieki wants to speak to you.'

'Goodbye, darling.' I felt unaccountably sad.

'Hello, Papa,' came Tieki's bright voice. 'I've got a new knife with lots of blades and things. The man in the *tere* party gave it to me.'

'You're a lucky boy, aren't you?'

'Yes, and it has something for removing stones from a horse's hoof.'

146

I laughed. 'That will be useful on Penrhyn, with all the horses there!'

'Don't be silly, Papa – there aren't any horses here.'

'Seahorses, perhaps.'

'Papa, be serious.'

'All right, I'm serious. What have you got to tell me?'

'Papa – it's about Mama.'

My God, I thought, it's true! All my worst fears came flooding back. She's seriously ill! 'What about Mama, Tieki?'

'She cries a lot, Papa.'

'Well,' I said, to reassure him and myself, 'she told me she was tired – the *tere* party took it out of her. So we mustn't show her we are worried – must we? Because that will make her more sad – and we don't want that, do we, darling?'

'No, Papa. I love you, Papa.'

'I love you, too.'

All the time I was on the phone, the Inspector was waiting patiently outside my door. I could see his bulky body through the frosted glass, and I felt resentful that he was about to take up more of my time. I just wanted to think about Tia. I'd been feeling low in spirits in the last few days. Did it have anything to do with Tia, and a premonition that she was seriously ill? And might the lines of poetry that came into my mind when I was walking along the avenue of flamboyants have been prompted by that knowledge? There was no question now of flying to New Zealand. I was needed back in Penrhyn. If only the bloody Inspector would let me go!

I opened the door and said, 'Sorry, Inspector – I was on the phone. Come in.'

'You'll have no more trouble from Miss Black,' he said, as he eased himself into a chair. 'I confronted her in her office with the kitchen knife, and warned her of the serious consequences if she didn't tell the truth, and she owned up, with a flood of tears. I'll have to charge her, of course, and she'll be fined quite a bit of money for wasting police time. She's been very stupid.'

147

'She'll never forgive me if she loses her job,' I said.

'That's a funny way of looking at it,' the Inspector said, giving me a puzzled look. 'You are more sinned against than sinning.'

'I'm certainly relieved,' I said, 'that her plot backfired. If she'd chosen a knife with a narrower blade, I might have been in trouble.'

'Only temporarily, perhaps,' said the Inspector. 'We have our sights on the real murderer.'

'And it's not Miss Black?'

'What do you think?'

'Well, if that's the case,' I said, 'why not let me go?' I was on the point of telling him that I was urgently needed back in Penrhyn, but refrained, because I have the superstitious feeling that if you keep dwelling on something you don't want to happen, you are sure to make it happen.

The Inspector broke into my thoughts. 'I think you should be free to go in two or three days.'

'Shall I ask Air New Zealand to keep a cancellation for me?' I asked.

The Inspector looked doubtful. 'Well, provisionally, anyway.'

After he had gone, I put a call through to Penrhyn for Tia's mother, Mere, to ring me, and then worked on my novel. The first call came from Air New Zealand, telling me they had a cancellation, and did I want it? I thanked the caller, and told her I'd have to pass it up – but to keep in touch with me. The second call was from Mere, and I was grateful that again there was little static.

'Ah, it's you, my son-in-law,' she shouted. 'My heart is glad you rang me. I was worried you wouldn't come back to our island – your mother's island, and yours too, now. Why you ring me, and not Tia?'

'I've already spoken to Tia,' I said, 'and it's you I want to talk to now.'

'You a funny boy,' she laughed. 'You never talk to me much in Penrhyn, and when you cross the sea you say to yourself I want to talk to Mere. What you want to talk to me about?'

I was surprised at her levity. 'I thought you might have something to tell me. Is everything all right?' I didn't like to ask her directly about Tia. If there was anything seriously wrong with her, I thought, Mere would surely tell me.

'Everything is good,' she said. 'The *tere* party has gone back to New Zealand, and we now talk about the good time we had – the prayer meetings in our new church hall, the *Biblia Tapu* discussions, and all the *himini* we sung. We are better people because of this.'

'No more hurricanes?' I said. 'You prayed that they keep away?' I was beginning to talk like her.

She laughed. 'Oh, yes – there was a hurricane that came near. But we prayed and it went away.'

'*Kapai* the prayer,' I said. We still hadn't got on to the subject of Tia, so I decided to take the bull by the horns, and said quite casually, 'And is Tia all right?'

Mere snorted. 'Oh, Tia – she fine! The silly girl she misses you, and she cries sometimes – that's all.'

'But,' I said, 'she told me she wasn't well, and Tieki told me the same.'

'Oh,' Mere cried, 'I know what that about. A *tere* party man he spend too much time with her. He talk to her, visit her, and it's not good. I tell him Tia a married woman – leave her alone.'

I didn't like the sound of that at all. Sidewinder with his usual vileness had accused her of being unfaithful, and what Mere was telling me increased rather than removed my feelings of doubt. 'And did he leave her alone?' I almost shouted, because I was beginning to feel fed up with everything.

'Oh, yes,' Mere shouted back. 'He stay away all right. Your Uncle Hiro he threatened to hit him if he didn't keep away.'

Good for him, I thought. I have never got on well with Uncle Hiro, so I was touched to hear he had protected my interests.

'Who is this fellow anyway?' I was angry because I couldn't help wondering how far the fellow had got, and that made me sick in the guts.

'Oh, his name is Tamati – he knew her long ago,' said Mere,

'before she marry the diplomat. They grew up together.'

Perhaps they were even lovers, I thought, disloyally. 'And did he stop seeing her?'

'He stop, all right – or Hiro beat him up.'

Hiro is a big man and quite capable of carrying out his threat.

'Tia worried sick about the man,' Mere went on, 'and the way he bothered her, but your uncle he stop all that nonsense.'

Yes, I thought, that would explain Tia's anxiety. She was worried sick that rumours would reach me about her having a fling with Tamati. I'm surprised she didn't tell me herself. Perhaps she felt guilty of unknowingly encouraging him. It must have been very difficult for her, and she couldn't face telling me.

I thanked Mere, and hung up. I should have been relieved, but all I thought about was some man's grubby hands on my wife. Doubt had taken root in my mind, and only Tia could pluck it out, but she was six hundred miles away, and unreachable except by the frustrating medium of the radio telephone. I wanted desperately to be with her, to talk this thing through with her, to make love with her.

The foul fiend chose this moment to appear. There he stood by the back door in his torn black velvet dress, his mouth open in an evil grin, his forked tongue flickering. 'Sucker!' he sneered. 'Of course, she's been tupped by Tamati, the black Porirua Ram. Naturally, she found him irresistible as all women do.'

'You bastard!' I yelled. 'You evil bastard!' I leapt out of my chair and attacked him, fists flailing, and, as usual, he showed his yellow streak. He squealed like a pig – which, after all, is one of his manifestations – and fell back, hands raised to protect his face.

'Admit it's a lie, go on,' I bawled, 'or I'll smash your face in.' I was really enjoying myself. I was getting rid of the grievances and frustrations I'd accumulated over the past week. The more I whacked him the better I felt, but I soon gave it up, disgusted with him and with myself, because I half believed his insinuations.

Breathing heavily, we stood facing each other. Then he had the cheek to stretch out a hand, and gently stroked my cheek, and then – most foul of all – he murmured in Tia's voice, 'Dear heart, we mustn't fight. We take too much out of each other. Ours is such a rare friendship.'

I spat in his face and shouted, 'I shit on your friendship!' and for a fraction of a second his face lit up with such fury I staggered back.

'My dear boy,' he murmured, immediately recovering, 'don't you see how it hurts me to see you suffer the pangs of jealous love. She's simply not worth it. No,' he said, raising his hand, 'don't thank me. I care for you. There's not a moment of the day when I don't think of you, worry about you. Sometimes I have the feelings of a wife for you.' As he said this, his face changed, and I saw Tia's face – not the real face that I knew and loved, but an evil caricature, twisted with lust and rage. He saw that I was horrified, changed back immediately, and murmured sadly, 'It's such a shame – such a lovely young woman, too.'

I was exhausted and said nothing. I closed my eyes, hoping desperately that if I ignored him he'd go away. But I should have known better. When I opened my eyes, he was standing in front of the mirror, preening and admiring himself. 'I really must take better care of myself. I'm so beautiful I could cry.'

At this I exploded with hysterical laughter. 'Beautiful – that's rich!' I snorted. 'Look at you. Don't you see how ridiculous you look in a dress. And what a dress! You look as if you've been dragged backards through a thornbush; it's got rips all over it.'

'It was that mutt of yours, 'he growled. 'I was making a peaceable visit when he pounced on me, without warning.' He glared at me. 'You put him up to it.' He suddenly sighed, and murmured, 'That's not the way to treat a friend.'

He saw me grinning and scowled, and revealed his true evil self. 'You'll be grinning on the other side of your face when I'm through with you. I fixed your mutt and before long I'll fix you.'

I laughed outright. 'You couldn't fix a – ' I didn't finish my sentence, because there came yet another knock on my door, and for once I was glad to be interrupted.

Sidewinder hissed, and out came the forked tongue, while the faint outline of green scales appeared on his face. With a tremendous effort he changed back, and became his smarmy self once more.

'It happens every time we are together,' he murmured, sadly. 'We are getting along swimmingly, everything looks perfect, then along comes some busybody and spoils it.' He wailed, 'Why do you do this to me?'

'Because you're a shit,' I shouted, just as the door swung open, and in came Miss Black, her large square face aflame.

'How dare you!' she shouted, her fists curled in anger.

'I wasn't talking to you.' I looked around, and was relieved to see that the fiend had disappeared.

'Oh,' she said, hands on hips. 'Are you in the habit of shouting obscenities at yourself?'

Equally angry, I shouted back, 'What are doing here, anyway? I didn't invite you in.'

'You didn't,' she said, uncertainly. 'I thought I heard you call, and naturally I assumed – '

'What do you want?' I asked, rudely.

'If you can't be civil,' she said, huffily, 'I'll go away.'

It was then that the mutt started barking. So Sidewinder couldn't have put paid to it! But why hadn't he warned me of the fiend's arrival? It sounded far away as before, as Miss Black swung her heavy head towards the back door, and listened intently.

'Is that a dog I hear?' She bit her thumb nervously. 'I thought I heard a dog. You haven't got a dog in the shower room, have you?'

I laughed, disdainfully. 'Of course I haven't got a dog in the shower room. What do you take me for?'

'I'm scared of dogs,' she mumbled. 'That dog that used to hang around the motel entrance, it scared me. It's gone now – and good riddance.'

Why is she so nervous? I wondered. The mutt barked again, and Miss Black got to her feet, ready for flight.

'Sit down, Miss Black,' I said as reasonably as I could. 'Say what you have come to say.'

'It sounded like the dog that used to frighten me,' she mumbled, as she sat down again. 'But, of course, it can't be – can it?' She was terribly nervous, twisting her handkerchief in her hand, like a child.

'What do *you* think?' I watched her closely. I felt the mutt wouldn't have barked, if she weren't a danger to me.

Those weirdly magnified eyes stared at me, as if trying to read my mind. 'Of course, it can't be,' she murmured.

'Get on with it.' I thought I had said it to myself, but I must have spoken aloud, because Miss Black stirred herself, and said, 'I have come to apologise to you for the stupid prank I played on you. I don't know what got into me.'

'I know,' I said, adding brutally, 'You're crazy, you know. The feud between our fathers is still festering in your mind, and you want to get at my father through me. Well, to hell with it. Bugger the sins of the fathers and all that. I'm not my father, and I don't see what you could have achieved by hanging the murder on me. But you made a mistake over the width of the blade, didn't you? Just as well you did, otherwise I might have been in deep trouble.'

She lifted her head on hearing this, and she actually smiled, a strange, almost seraphic smile, with a touch – yes – of evil in it.

Simultaneously the mutt started up again, and this time there was no mistaking the warning note in his bark.

I have to admit it. She scared me, sitting there, smiling secretly, and I wanted her out of my room as quickly as possible.

'Look,' I said, getting to my feet, 'I accept your apology. Now I must get on with my writing.' I showed her to the door, and all the time she was smiling her secret smile.

'Abyssinia Samoa,' she murmured, as I closed the door on her.

CHAPTER ELEVEN

I DIDN'T HAVE a good night's rest. I dreamt that the motel was some kind of concentration camp with a high, barbed wire fence all round it nailed to coconut trees. All of us inmates had our own rooms, and were free to wander about inside the compound, but no one was ever allowed outside. None of us even knew why we were prisoners, we hadn't committed any crimes we knew of. We weren't political prisoners, radicals, or any kind of activist.

I had complained to the commandant, Inspector Twinkel-baum, and all he did was wink at me, and call in Miss Black, the head warder, who wore glasses as huge as dinner plates, which magnified her eyes so grotesquely she looked like some bug from outer space. She took off her glasses and wiped them, and I was amazed to see her eyes shrink to tiny holes out of which squeezed little tears like pearls.

Twinkelbaum kept winking at me, while Miss Black muttered, 'Dear, dear, this will never do. I must have discipline, I must have discipline!'

The Inspector whispered to me, his massive hand covering his mouth, 'I told you – she should never have been allowed to run the motel. She's too bossy. She upsets the inmates.' He looked very smug, as he sat back in his chair, which creaked alarmingly under his weight.

'What do you suggest we do? You're the number one suspect now. You tell us.'

'I didn't think I was the number one suspect any more.' And I burst into tears.

'Here,' shouted Miss Black, 'stop that. Suspects aren't allowed to cry.'

'Not on their first day anyway,' corrected the Inspector, his mouth pursed like an ovipositor. 'He hasn't been here long enough.'

'I've been here a week,' I shouted, wailing louder than ever.

The Inspector looked deeply concerned, and drummed the table with his fingers. 'This is very serious.'

'It is bloody serious,' Miss Black agreed. 'But I shouldn't ask the suspect for advice.'

'Nor I,' said the Inspector. 'It's much too early to ask him. He might give us bad advice. It's been known to happen.'

'Oh, indeed it has,' said Miss Black, frowning thoughtfully. 'But how long is long enough? That's what I'd like to know.'

'That's what we'd all like to know,' said the Inspector, who got up and bowed.

'May I make a suggestion?' I asked, putting up my hand.

'What's he saying?' bawled the Inspector, sitting down and cupping an ear with his hand.

'Oh,' growled Miss Black, 'take no notice of him. I think he's a trouble-maker.'

'Have you ever thought,' I grumbled, 'that I might want to leave the room?'

'Leave the room,' snapped Miss Black. 'What impertinence! It will be leave the motel next – and where will that leave us then?'

'He's a tricky one,' said the Inspector, eyeing me narrowly.

'Tricky's right,' said Miss Black, and seeing me raise my hand, she shouted, 'No – you may not leave the room.'

'Are you addressing me?' muttered the Inspector, crossly. 'Look I can't see without my glasses – lend me yours.' And he made a swipe at Miss Black's glasses, but she smacked his hand.

'Now you've done it,' he muttered, lifting his hand to his mouth and sucking it. 'This is serious.' He shouted at me. 'What's the number one suspect got to say to that?'

'I say nothing,' I shouted back.

'What's wrong with the fellow?' grumbled the Inspector. 'He shouts at us, but has nothing to say.'

'Oh,' I shouted again, 'that's where you're wrong. I've got plenty to say.'

'What's he saying now?' grumbled the Inspector. 'I've never

known such a talkative fellow. It passes comprehension.'

'I was good at comprehension at school,' I volunteered shyly.

'Maybe,' said Miss Black, 'but you can be too clever.'

'If I was really clever,' I pointed out, slyly, 'I wouldn't be here now, would I?'

'What's the beggar saying now?' complained the Inspector, bending an ear towards her.

Miss Black glared at me. 'I think he wants to escape.'

'Escape! He must be mad. There's no escape – doesn't he know that? A clever fellow like him.'

'He knows little about anything, I'm afraid,' muttered Miss Black. 'That's why he's here.'

'That's why we're all here,' said the Inspector, glumly, then brightened up. 'But at least I've solved the murder.'

'What murder?' I shouted.

'There he goes shouting again,' muttered the Inspector. He addressed me stiffly. 'It will get you nowhere, you know. You'll not get special privileges.'

'That's the trouble with weekend writers,' yelled Miss Black. 'They all want special privileges.'

'Weekend writers!' I exploded. 'Who are you calling a weekend writer?'

'You, as a matter of fact,' she said, calmly. 'That's my considered opinion.'

'But, don't you see, I solved the murder,' insisted the Inspector.

'What murder?' muttered Miss Black, deeply offended.

'I asked that first,' I shouted. 'Fair's fair.'

'Well,' said the Inspector, shaking his head at Miss Black. 'He did, you know.'

Miss Black thrust out her jaw. 'Well, answer it then – and stop pussyfooting around.'

The Inspector slapped his knee and laughed. 'I was coming to that.'

That's when I woke up. Can you understand why I'm terrified of the irrational? It's always my luck to be cooped up in a nuthouse taken over by the inmates, and it's too bad that I can't escape them even in dreams. But of one thing I'm pretty sure. The Inspector has solved the murder, but is saying nothing until all the pieces fit neatly together, and that might take a little more time. He has some funny idea I hold the key, but don't know it.

I didn't hear the mutt last night, so there couldn't have been any unwelcome visitors, unless of course Sidewinder muzzled him again. I hope not. In the deadly fight ahead, I could well do with his services.

The phone rang while I was having breakfast in my room. It was Dr Ruby's nurse, who said, '*Kia orana*, Dr Ruby would like to talk to you.'

'But I thought Dr Ruby was at a medical conference in Canberra.'

'That's Dr Richard Ruby. It's Dr Marie Ruby who wants to talk to you.'

I'd forgotten it was a husband and wife practice. I wonder what she wants.

'Good morning,' said Dr Marie Ruby, a light pleasant voice. 'I hope I haven't struck you at an inconvenient time. If so, tell me, and I'll ring back later.'

'No, it's all right.'

'I am having a few people round for drinks this evening, and I wondered if you would care to come along. It will be quite casual – nothing too grand, and you might find an answer to your problem.'

What's she on about? I wondered. But as I hadn't planned anything for the evening I decided to accept. 'Thank you – I'd like to come. What time?'

'Oh, around five.'

After she rang off, I decided to ring Tia, and found her tired, cautious, and a little on the defensive.

'Hello, darling,' she said, 'it's so lovely to hear your voice. I hope you are going to tell me that the Inspector is going to let you go at last.'

'No – not yet, but he will very soon, I feel.'

'Isn't he the limit!'

There was a burst of static, and I knew that the fiend was up to his old tricks. His nose must be badly out of joint over his failure to push Tamati into Tia's bed and so break up our marriage, and he was determined to destroy our conversation by making communication impossible. We were accordingly subjected to a variety of hideous sounds – screeching, caterwauling, hysterical laughter, and the like – until even he got bored with his mischief-making, and abandoned it, and Tia and I could hear ourselves again.

'I don't like the sound of that at all.' Tia was tense and troubled, but not, I was pleased to hear, afraid, and this made me wonder if she had been aware of Sidewinder all along, but had pushed him to the back of her mind. It was beginning to look that way. Perhaps it was this knowledge that was making her ill rather than the unwanted attentions of a womaniser, insensitive to the distress and hostility he might be causing. I was filled with foreboding.

'Are you there, darling?' Tia sounded tearful, and very far away.

'I'm sorry, love,' I said, quietly. 'I had something on my mind. 'No – I don't like it either. There's probably a storm somewhere – that's all.'

'Mama told me you rang her,' came her wavering voice. 'She said you were worried about me.'

'Yes, dear, I was worried about you. When you told me you weren't well – '

'I shouldn't have told you that,' she interrupted. 'It was a selfish thing to do.' She paused, then went on, hesitantly, 'There was, this man, you see – '

'You needn't tell me,' I said quickly, 'that is, if you don't want to.'

'Oh, but I do want to,' she said, quietly. 'I must tell you for my peace of mind.'

'But you didn't do any wrong,' I pointed out. 'You didn't

encourage him. From what Mere said, he made a nuisance of himself and kept bothering you.'

'We used to be lovers,' she said, a sob in her voice.

Oh, God, I thought – here it comes! Why does she think she has to confess. I'd rather not know. We all have skeletons in our cupboards, and that's where they should stay.

'I've been thinking about this,' Tia went on, 'until I nearly went out of my head, and I decided I had to tell you. It happened long ago when we were children. It's our Island way that children should discover sex before marriage. It's not wrong.'

'I know,' I said, crudely. 'It's off into the bushes and down with the pants. You have already told me about that. Sure, it makes sense.'

'You see,' Tia said, sadly. 'You *are* hurt. That's why I didn't tell you yesterday on the phone. I thought we'd talk about it when you came home.'

'And that's all there was to it?' I said, trying to keep the harshness out of my voice.

'That's all.' She was very subdued.

'No rekindling of the old flame?'

'None.'

'Not even the slightest flicker?' Fool that I am – I wanted to hurt her! So I kept needling her. 'Did you know that your ex-lover is known as Tamati the Porirua Ram?'

'Why are you doing this to me?' she cried, a note of anger in her voice. 'It's all over and done with. I don't think of Tamati in that way any more - and it's unkind to call him that. He's not a bad man.'

'No – but he had the hots for you!' I was merciless.

Tia was angry. 'That's a disgusting expression!'

'It may be disgusting, but it happens to be true. He had it all worked out – a knife for Tieki, a poke for you, and a knife in the back for me. '

Tia went quiet, and then said, 'This is a side of you I haven't seen before. I didn't know it existed, and I don't like it. It makes me unhappy.'

'You aren't meant to like it,' I snapped, then I suddenly felt cheap and flat, utterly disgusted with myself. I knew she was what I could never be – totally loyal and honest. I suspected that the flame might have flickered, but what of it? It's a normal enough reaction in a healthy young woman temporarily parted from her husband, and this knowledge may have contributed to her distress. But I couldn't hold that against her, when my own behaviour was so suspect. If I were frank, I would tell her that Naomi had aroused me, and that I couldn't be sure how far I would have gone, if Paula hadn't turned up and claimed her.

But even if I had told her, she would have blamed Naomi and not me, saying that it was she who tempted me – which of course she had – and as nothing had happened, what was there to feel guilty about? I'm sure she rejects, as I do, the old puritan ethic that you can commit adultery in the mind as in the flesh.

'Can you hear me, darling?' came Tia's plaintive voice. 'Oh, dear – it's hopeless trying to carry on a discussion by radio telephone. That's why I wanted to wait until you came home. Darling, what's happened is what I feared would happen. You're upset, and so am I. Believe me – I've done nothing to be ashamed of.'

'I know that,' I shouted above the static.

'I love you so much,' came her wailing reply, distorted by interference.

'I love you, too,' and I was about to beg her forgiveness when the sound waves suddenly exploded in maniacal laughter.

'What was that awful laughter?' There was horror in her voice.

I didn't know what appalled me more – Tia's hearing Side-winder's voice for the first time, or the fiend hanging around in his sneaky way, and gloating over our little spat, before blowing it away with mocking laughter.

What am I to do? Pretend I didn't hear it? Or take Tia into my confidence, and tell her that the fiend had been pursuing me for years, and wouldn't be satisfied until he had gained possession of my soul. But I didn't have to do either. Tia had unconsciously been aware of Sidewinder all along, and now that the crisis was near, this knowledge, so to speak, had risen to the surface of her mind. She was appalled at the danger I was in, and didn't hesitate to take my side.

'What else could I do?' she asked me later. 'I love you, and when you love someone, you don't have a choice, do you?'

But I am anticipating. Loud static had followed the fiend's crazy laughter, and as communication was now out of the question, we screamed above the static, 'I love you,' and hung up.

I had the whole day ahead of me, and although it was raining, I went for a walk to Black Rock. I like nothing better than to walk in the rain in the tropics. I never wear a raincoat, but walk out in what I happen to be wearing – on this occasion, a shirt, shorts, and jandals – and let the rain soak me through. I find it soothing. I try not to dwell on my worries, but walk along with the same careless freedom I enjoyed as a child. I know my clothes will dry out in a matter of minutes when the sun comes out.

The rain became heavier as I approached Black Rock. I could see it pimpling the rockpools on the reef, and I suddenly wanted to swim in one of the deeper pools surrounding the rocks. As children, my sister and I had spent many happy hours in its clear lukewarm water, and there were many times our mother had to send our nanny, an Island girl not much older than ourselves, to tell us to come home.

There were people at the rock. I could hear the shrill tones of a girl and the deeper ones of a man, and I felt resentful – I had wanted the pool to myself – and I was about to retrace my steps, when the girl saw me and called out.

'Come and join us. It's lovely.' It was the blonde girl from the motel, and beside her stood the bodybuilder, resplendent in his nakedness, having pumped up his muscles. The girl, too, was naked, and was a fine physical specimen, as she stood there smiling, her full breasts cupped by the water.

'Don't know if I will,' I said, fatuously. 'I haven't brought my togs.'

'Don't be silly,' she laughed. 'Slip off your things and come in – or, if you prefer, come in as you are.'

I didn't know whether to tell them that appearing naked in public is frowned on, and can even lead to unpleasantness, but I decided it wasn't my business – let them enjoy themselves.

I took off my shirt and shorts, but left my underpants on, and dived into the pool.

'My – aren't you a shy one!' she laughed, when I came to the surface, blowing bubbles. She began splashing me with water, and soon all three of us were behaving like great kids, but when I saw that the bodybuilder had developed an erection, and seemed more interested in leap-frogging over me than over the girl, I decided it was time I left them to it.

'See you back at the motel,' I said, climbing out of the pool.

'Sure,' said the bodybuilder, looking crestfallen, but the girl had lost interest in me, and was drawing his lips down to hers with one hand, and sheathing his mighty sword – *pace* Cleland – with the other.

That evening the young people in the motel talked in shocked tones of the vicious assault and rape of two of their mates. It must have occurred soon after I left them. It appears that four youths were mooching along the road, which comes close to the pool at this point, when one of them happened to hear the girl's cry of pleasure. He decided to investigate, and when he saw the pair having sex, he called to the others, and all four stole down the bank and surprised them. They beat the young man senseless, and knocked the girl about before raping her. Her screams were heard by a passing cyclist, but he valued his skin too much, and kept riding. He reported the incident to the police, but it's unlikely, given the circumstances, that the culprits will be caught.

Would it have made any difference, I wondered, if I'd warned them? I had my doubts. The girl was the dominant one, and she struck me as wilful and headstrong, and would probably have laughed at me.

At five o'clock, I walked through a small banana grove to Dr Ruby's surgery. It was still raining, but so lightly it merely dampened my shirt. Several cars passed me, one of them a posh red Mercedes, with the Japanese couple sitting upright in the back seat. The man was wearing a dark suit and tie, and his wife was equally severe in a black dress. I noticed these details, because I had taken Dr Ruby's advice to heart and decided to turn up in the clothes I'd worn to Black Rock.

I certainly looked out of place among those visiting and local worthies, some of whom were dressed to the nines, and all were looking cross and uncomfortable.

Dr Ruby drifted towards me, smiling. 'How nice of you to come,' she murmured, stretching out an elegant hand, fingers drooping, and I didn't know whether she wanted me to kiss it or shake it. But it wasn't intended for me anyway, but for the German couple from the motel who were behind me. They had arrived a little after me, in a rusty taxi, driven by my countryman Muscles, who, the reader may remember, had driven me and the Nuggetts to the motel on our arrival in Rarotonga. He hadn't declared his hand, so I didn't know whether he was for me, or against me.

Ah, Dr Ruby had noticed me at last! She was an extraordinary looking woman, with bright red spiky hair, an electric blue dress, and an imitation shark's-tooth necklace of stainless steel.

'I'm so glad you could come,' she said. 'My daughter is studying your poems at school, and I do so like them, because they are so *real*.' As she prattled on, talking non-stop, I wondered if she spoke like this on all occasions, or only on social occasions.

'Here's my daughter now,' she burbled, thrusting a large sulky girl, with a similar shock of red hair, towards me. 'Oenone, darling – I want you to meet the poet whose poems you so much like.'

The girl scowled at me, and I couldn't help noticing she would have been very attractive, if she could have straightened herself, held her head up, and stopped pulling faces.

'She plans to be an anthropologist one day,' the proud mother declared. That must explain her shapeless mother–hubbard dress, I thought.

'Can I go now, Mother?' she said, aggressively. She had cultivated a deep voice, and again I thought she'd have a really attractive speaking voice, if she'd only speak normally.

'Oh, I thought you'd want to meet your favourite poet.'

'He's not my favourite poet,' Oenone growled. 'I don't have a favourite poet.'

'What class are you in, Enemy?' I chipped in.

The girl glared at me, and then laughed, and her face became charged with real beauty. 'There you are, Mother. I told you it was a rotten name. You shouldn't have given it to me.'

'It was your father's idea – not mine,' Dr Ruby said. 'He took it from a poem by Tennyson – a favourite of his.'

'Please, Mother, may I go now?' she said, thrusting out her chin, but I was glad to see there was a twinkle in her eyes.

'All right, then, but what do you say to the poet?'

The girl gave me a mocking little bow, and said, 'Please to meet you, I'm sure.' And ran off.

Dr Ruby looked after her and frowned. 'Sometimes I'm half out of my wits not knowing what to do with her.' Then she turned to me and said, 'Do you have any children? Oh, what am I saying – I do beg your pardon.'

'It's all right,' I said. 'I have an adopted son – and there are two little girls, twins, and a baby girl, my wife and I have more or less adopted.'

She looked at me with a professional eye, and I was amused to see that her voice had also changed and had become more business-like.

'I wonder if I can have a word with you in private?' She piloted me through the crowd into a small conservatory, off the veranda, where we found Oenone sitting in a cane chair and reading a book of verse, and I wondered if it was mine.

'Oops,' she said. 'I'm not here.' And she ducked out a side

164

door, with a nervous giggle.

'Do you remember ringing my husband, oh, about six months ago from Penrhyn?' asked Dr Ruby. 'Yes, of course, you do. The static was so bad – it generally is, I suppose.'

'Yes, I remember.' I certainly did. I'd tried to shout above the static, but all I succeeded in doing was to attract a large number of idlers, who found listening to me shouting my inability to impregnate my wife high drama compared with the monotonous routine of daily life in the Northern Cooks.

'Well, my husband,' Dr Ruby went on, 'did get the gist of what you were trying to say – he told me about it afterwards. He was going to ring you about it – but you know how it is. He's involved in so many things he didn't find the time. But I've invited you here to meet one of the guests at your motel, who's a specialist in the field.'

I wondered who that could be.

'Wait here,' she said, pressing my hand. 'I'll bring him to you.'

When her mother went out, Oenone came in shyly and asked me to sign the book she was reading. It was, as I'd suspected, a copy of an early book of mine.

'Do you write poems?' I asked her, as I signed the book.

'I try to,' she said, 'but I'm not very good.'

'Give yourself time,' I told her, 'there's no hurry.'

'When did you start writing?'

'About your age.'

She smiled, transforming her rather sallow face. 'I may have a chance yet.'

'Stick to it, read good poets, and if you have the gift there's no reason why you can't become a good poet yourself.'

'*If* I have the gift – I don't know that I have.'

'You'll know.'

She thanked me, and ran out, as her mother returned with the specialist, who was none other than the Japanese gentleman who was staying at the motel with his wife. She introduced him as Professor Shiki.

I should explain at this point that I'd had a prostate operation in New Zealand which made it impossible for me to give Tia a baby. Sidewinder, whom I'd first encountered in a psychiatric hospital, knew of my condition, and thought he could turn it to his advantage. He actually had the gall to propose that a fellow demon, Beelzebub, assume my form, and impregnate Tia, without her being aware of the subterfuge. He added insult to injury, when he said, sneeringly, that Beelzebub would satisfy my wife better than I ever could. I felt like smashing him in the face.

It shows you how out of touch he is with ordinary decency that he can point to Attila the Hun, Hitler and Stalin, as advertisements of similar deals he has made in the past. The price, of course, was to be my 'spotty little soul', as he called it in a moment of bitterness.

Anyway, I've kept Professor Shiki waiting long enough. Not that I needed an introduction. We have bumped into each other on numerous occasions at the motel, and each time he has bowed and smiled thinly.

'Professor Shiki,' Dr Ruby was saying, 'is a distinguished urologist in his own country – and he's right here. Isn't that a co-incidence? I've told him of your little problem' – I squirmed at that – 'and he said he'd be honoured to be of service to you.'

'Honoured!' I looked at the professor, and his mouth was a straight line under his pencil-thin moustache. I couldn't decide whether it indicated approval or distaste.

'Of course I'll pay you,' I said, in my rough Kiwi manner.

He winced, and murmured in a high-pitched voice, 'I wouldn't hear of it.' He turned to Dr Ruby and said, 'If you care to return to your guests, Dr Ruby, I shall talk to this young man alone.' Did I see a glint in his eye, because I was sure he was younger than me, and he knew it.

We sat down in the cane chairs, and he asked me a number of questions, such as when did I have the prostatectomy, where did I have it done, who the surgeon was, how old was I, was I able to father children before the operation, and so on. I'm a squeamish fellow, and I was acutely aware that the schoolgirl might be lurking outside, drinking in this highly personal information.

I was able to answer all his questions satisfactorily, including one relating to my fertility. I told Professor Shiki I'd had an affair with a young woman in Wellington, and that she had conceived, and had flown to Melbourne to have it terminated. She never told me about it until several years later, when we bumped into each other in Cuba Mall.

Professor Shiki waited patiently until I finished my recital, but a flicker in his eyes suggested that my choice of the word 'bumped' might have been a trifle indelicate. I suppose you'd call him a Japanese 'exquisite'.

'Of course,' he murmured, in his high-pitched voice, that made him sound like a precocious child, 'you must understand that the operation cannot be reversed to give normal ejaculation.'

'You mean,' I said, 'that I can never ejaculate normally as I could before the operation?'

He nodded and murmured, 'That's precisely what I do mean. What happens now is that you ejaculate into your bladder. There are techniques whereby the sperm can be collected from the bladder and transferred to your wife to fertilise her ovum.'

He went on to give me additional information of a more technical nature, but I had learnt all I needed to know, and I felt so happy I could have shouted for joy. I couldn't wait to ring Tia and give her the good news.

'And my wife and I would need to have it done in hospital?' I said, excitedly.

He winced again when I used the expression 'have it done', but he again gave a delicate nod of his head, and murmured, 'Ideally, yes, both of you would need to spend a little time in hospital where the techniques could be properly applied.'

I thanked Professor Shiki profusely, and hurried out of the conservatory, remembered my manners and went back, and then accompanied him to the veranda where the guests were showing signs of merriment.

Dr Ruby came forward, looked at me, her eyebrows raised in a query.

'Professor has been very helpful,' I told her, 'and I'm really grateful to you for bringing us together.'

'Well,' she said, with a smile, 'it's the least I could do. My husband felt guilty that he didn't get back to you.' Then she took my arm and said, 'Now I'd like you to meet some of the other guests.'

'If you don't mind, Dr Ruby,' I murmured, 'I'd like to hurry back to the motel to ring my wife and give her the good news.'

'Are you sure? You could telephone her from here.'

'I'd rather not. There are a lot of personal details I want to explain to her, and I'd like to do so in private.'

'I understand.' But Dr Ruby was able to introduce me to a few of the guests, one of whom, a Minister of the Crown, looked askance at my shorts and jandals. I remembered him from an earlier visit to Rarotonga when he had kicked up over my wearing jandals to an official function. He was a heavy drinker, and a dangerous driver, and as we weaved through the narrow streets of the island, his wife and I practically clung together, fearful we'd have an accident and be killed.

Near the door, the German woman, whom, you may remember, I suspected of being a witch, plucked at my sleeve, and hissed, 'Beware of the snake demon.'

'What?' I stammered, startled out of my wits.

'You heard.'

Oenone came out of the conservatory, holding up my book, and pointing at it with her other hand, and smiling.

Muscles was sitting in his taxi at the top of the drive, and when he saw me, he got out and said, 'I've been waiting for you.'

'But I didn't ring for a taxi,' I said.

'No – but I thought you might want a lift to your motel. I'm declaring myself.'

'What?' I felt dizzy with happiness.

'I thought you'd like to know,' said Muscles. 'I'm declaring myself. I'm in your corner.'

168

Muscles dropped me off at the motel entrance, and as soon as I went through the front door I knew something out of the ordinary had happened. There was a sense of simmering excitement affecting staff and guests.

I went into the bar where Tere was serving, and I found that he, too, could hardly contain himself.

'What on earth has happened, Tere?'

'Haven't you heard, chief?'

'Heard what?'

'Miss Black, she's been arrested for murder.'

'But that's unbelievable.' My head was spinning. 'But I thought the Inspector has already cleared her of the murder.'

'Not any more, he ain't, chief.' Tere wiped the bar in front of me, and said, 'A stubby, is it?'

'No thanks, Tere,' I said. 'I've got a lot on my mind, and I want to sort it out in my room.'

'Sure – catch you later.'

The news of the arrest had certainly brought me down to earth with a thump. Back in my room, feeling subdued, I rang the telephone exchange and asked the operator to put me through to Tia in Penrhyn.

'There's a lot of interference this evening, sir, but I'll do what I can.'

'That's all I ask.'

A few minutes later, she rang back, and said the static had got much worse. Did I want her to keep trying? I swallowed my disappointment, thanked her, and asked her to try again in the morning.

'What time, sir?'

'Any time after six.'

Then utterly exhausted, I lay on my bed in my clothes, and dropped into a hole, and slept. And as I slept, news broke of the vicious rape at Black Rock, but as I have already described it I shall let it lie, and press on with my story.

169

I WOKE UP to the shattering sound of the telephone. I groaned, switched on the bedside lamp, heaved myself out of bed, stumbled to the phone, and picked it up, expecting to hear Tia at the other end.

'Is that you, darling?' I shouted, assuming there'd be interference on the air waves.

'That's the first time I've been called darling since my wife died.' It was the Inspector in a sardonic mood.

'My God, Inspector,' I shouted. 'Why are you ringing at this ungodly hour?' I looked at my watch. 'It's three o'clock.'

'There's no need to shout, sir. I may be your darling – but I'm not deaf.'

'Inspector, stop playing games, and tell me what you want.'

'You may know,' he said, calmly, 'I arrested Miss Black in connection with the murder of Bela Roll.'

'Yes, yes – I know that,' I muttered, impatiently. 'Come to the point. Roll, is that her surname? I never knew that.'

'Well, sir – I'm ringing to warn you that she has escaped from custody.'

'What's that got to do with me?' I grumbled. 'It's a small island. You'll have no trouble – what's the word? – apprehending her.'

'It's more serious than that,' the Inspector said. 'It appears she has a violent hatred for you. I thought you should know.'

I didn't like the sound of that at all, and I liked it even less when he mentioned she had stolen an axe from the police station and, in her state of mind, must be considered a danger to society.

'You mean me, don't you, Inspector?' I muttered, looking at the back door, and half-expecting the mad woman to burst through, waving the axe. 'You're suggesting she's out to get me – isn't that why you rang?'

'Hang on there – don't get carried away.'

'Inspector,' I said, raising my voice, 'if I don't get police protection – I'll get carried away all right – in a box.'

'I don't think it's as serious as that.' He actually sounded amused.

'Why do you think she stole the axe – to cut firewood? Inspector, if it's not as serious as that, why did you ring me at three in the morning?'

'I suggest you take the ordinary precautions – lock your windows and doors – and you'll be safe enough.'

'There you go again,' I spluttered. 'You use the word "safe", which suggests to me that I'm far from safe.'

'Good night, sir,' he said, wearily. 'As I said, take the normal precautions and you'll be all right.'

The Inspector hung up, and then, as if at a signal, the mutt started barking loudly outside my back door. I ran and locked it, and secured it with the chain, then locked the front door and all the windows. As an added precaution, I jammed the backs of chairs under the door knobs, then waited, sweat running from my face and body.

Think, think! I urged myself. Find a weapon, defend yourself! But my mind had seized up, as waves of panic swept over me. Run, run! went the voice in my head. For God's sake – run for your life!

I ran to the front door, and opened it just as the back door burst open, scattering glass across the room, and I saw Miss Black, eyes starting out of her head, standing in the doorway, axe in hand, blood running down her face from cuts made by flying glass.

On seeing me, she smiled, but it was a smile so false and crazy, I shuddered. 'Ah, there you are,' she crooned. 'Stay, don't run away.' But the way she held the axe, head raised, belied her words. She noticed my alarm, and at once put down the axe on a chair. 'See,' she murmured, 'I don't mean you any harm.' She took a step forward, and leered, 'We have so much in common, you and I!'

I found her wheedling tones much more horrible than screams of pure hatred. 'Don't come any closer,' I yelled, every muscle in my body ready for flight.

'Don't be like that,' she pleaded, her hands held out in a gesture of peace. But she could see I wasn't taken in. She narrowed her eyes, suddenly grabbed the axe, and made a lunge at me.

I was expecting such an attack. I slipped out the door, and slammed it shut behind me, just as the axe, swung with enormous power, smashed through it, showering the path with splintered wood and glass.

I can tell you I ran for my life, while Miss Black, roaring like an enraged buffalo, thundered after me.

If I could have thought clearly, I would have been very amused, because the situation had all the elements of a farce. But it's not easy to be detached when a fifteen stone female pursues you, waving an axe, and yelling blue murder.

I don't know what possessed me, but I decided that the safest place for me would be up a coconut tree. She couldn't get at me there, I figured. As a boy I had often escaped my father's wrath by hiding among the fronds and bunches of coconut at the top of a young tree in our garden in Takuvaine Road, coming down only when he had been pacified by my mother.

It was this tree I headed for, forgetting that thirty years had passed since I last climbed it. When I reached it, I found it was twice the height it was then. But Miss Brown was closing in, and I had no alternative but to climb it. I was halfway up when she reached the base, and tried to shake it, bellowing at me, between sucking in deep gulps of air, to be sensible and come down. But I kept climbing, and the higher I got the more scared I became. The top seemed no nearer, while the base, with Miss Black glaring up at me, seemed far away.

She began her wheedling again. 'Do come down. I just want to talk about the old days. Be sensible – I won't hurt you.'

It was a darkish night, with just enough light on the axe head to make it glint, so I declined her invitation, and kept climbing.

This made her so angry that she took to the tree with the axe, whacking it so powerfully it shook.

'For Christ's sake,' I bawled. 'What are you doing?'

'Come down,' she panted, 'and I'll tell you. I only want a word with you. Surely you can spare me that!'

What was I to do? If I continued climbing she could cut the tree down and I'd fall and break my neck, but if I climbed down she might attack me with the axe. I was between the devil and the deep blue sea.

But fortunately for me help was on the way. Miss Black had made so much noise she had woken up the neighbourhood. Lights had come on in all the houses roundabout, and people were coming on to the street to investigate. The police had also been rung, and I heard the siren coming closer and closer, and stop outside the gate.

'Look what you've done,' wailed Miss Black. 'We won't be able to have our little talk now. I hope you're satisfied.' She sounded like a disappointed child.

But I couldn't move. I was paralysed with fear. My arms were stuck to the tree, and I knew that if I moved I would fall.

'You can come down now.' It was the Inspector, and I thought I detected amusement in his voice. 'We have Miss Black – you have nothing more to fear from her.'

'I can't move, Inspector,' I called down to him. 'I'm stuck. You'll have to bring a ladder, or call the fire brigade.' Worse was to come. It began to rain, and the bark soon became slippery, and difficult to grip. I don't know how I conquered my fear. I must have shut off my mind, and let the instinct for survival take over. Before I knew what I was doing, I had slithered down the trunk, and fallen in an exhausted heap at its base, just as Tai and Fred came running up with an extension ladder.

'Not needed now, thanks,' said the Inspector, as he pulled me to my feet. 'Well, you certainly attract trouble, don't you?' He grinned as he slapped me on the shoulder.

'How comforting it must be to you to see humour in other

people's misfortune,' I said, sarcastically. 'If I had slipped I would have been killed.'

'I'm sorry,' he said. 'These last few days have been quite a strain – '

'You can say that again, Inspector,' I grumbled.

'And I'm feeling a little light-headed. Come along to the station, and I'll get you a cup of tea.'

'I'd sooner be in bed.'

'Don't you want to know how we came to arrest Miss Black?'

'I think I already know.'

'Well, aren't you a bright one,' he muttered, but I wasn't sure whether he meant it, or was being sarcastic.

This is my big moment, I told myself, as we walked to the waiting police car, where Miss Black was sitting in the back, weeping quietly beside Fred.

'Take her in, Tai,' the Inspector said, 'and see that's she's locked in properly. We don't want another late night charade.' As Tai got in behind the wheel, the Inspector asked him, 'What have you done with the axe?'

'I chucked it in the boot.'

'Good man! Well, off you go then.' The Inspector slapped the roof of the car, and as it drew away he turned to me and said, 'I'll walk you home. I could do with some exercise before I turn in. And there's nothing nicer than walking in the early morning – the air is fresh, and everything is clean and sparkling.'

We walked in silence for a while, then he said, 'Let's hear it then.'

'I don't know if I can gather my thoughts together,' I said. 'But I'll give it a go.'

'Fire away.'

'Well, there's the business of the blades. It occurred to me that Miss Black was being too subtle when she planted the kitchen knife in my room. But she planted it there not so much to put the heat on me as to take it off herself. I asked myself why the big blade? It's a very big knife, and I couldn't see her carrying it around, waiting for the opportunity to use it. Also she took the knife from the kitchen where, as manager, her presence wouldn't normally be remarked on. But on this occasion she made sure she was seen taking it.

'You were supposed to think like this. If she had been the killer, she would have known that the murder weapon had a narrow blade and would have planted such a knife in my room, which would have put me on the spot. But, by planting a knife with a broad blade, she showed she had no idea what type of blade had been used: ergo, she's innocent.' I paused and asked, 'Does any of this make sense?'

The Inspector's eyes gleamed in the early light. 'Perhaps – go on.'

'I think I suspected Miss Black from the moment I remembered seeing her pottering about the pool after the first time Bela left me. You jogged my memory – remember?' The Inspector nodded. 'Obviously, I couldn't prove it, but I believe Miss Black and Bela quarrelled when Bela got back to her room, and it upset her so much she ran to my room to get away from Miss Black. When Bela returned, they quarrelled again, and Miss Black killed her in a fit of jealousy. She may have been thinking about killing her for some time and had the knife on her. I believe they were lovers.' The Inspector was so quiet I wondered if he'd been listening. 'Do you want me to go on?'

'Certainly – I'm impressed.'

It was still too dark to see the expression on his face, so I couldn't be sure whether he was sincere, or laughing at me.

'There's not much more,' I said. 'But I have a number of thoughts you may find interesting.' I paused for a comment from him, but as he remained quiet I continued. I mentioned Naomi and Paula from New Zealand, suggesting that these two women, plus Bela and Miss Black, belonged to a witches' coven. I suggested that the German might also be a member, because she was undoubtedly a witch.

'I found no evidence,' said the Inspector, 'that there was a coven. However, I'm certain the four women were connected in some way. In fact, Miss Black has been seen in the company of Naomi and Paula, but an enquiry hasn't shown that they are implicated in the killing, or even that they knew or suspected that Miss Black was the killer. As for the German lady,' he chuckled, 'well, you'll find witches anywhere. This may be a good season for them.' He laughed. 'No, she's not implicated in any way.'

I suppose I was naive to think that the Inspector would share his thoughts with me. But he did tell me that they had found the knife, and that all the evidence pointed to Miss Black's guilt. I might mention here, because developments in my life were to drive the case out of my mind, that Miss Black was never brought to trial. She committed suicide in prison. Someone, possibly Naomi or Paula, managed to slip her a bottle of Halcion tablets, and she swallowed the lot, and was found dead next morning with the empty bottle beside her.

It was five o'clock when I got back to my unit, and I was glad to put my head down, even though I knew that my kip could only be a short one. And so it turned out. Promptly at six the phone rang and I lifted the receiver, expecting to hear my darling Tia's voice, but heard instead Sidewinder's hateful and mocking voice.

'I'm so sorry to disappoint you. You expected to hear Tia's voice, didn't you?'

'Get off the bloody line,' I shouted. 'I don't want to talk to you.'

'You know,' he went on, imperturbably, 'Miss Black has been a great disappointment to me. I rather hoped she would have done for you. I gave her the axe, pointed her in the right direction, but what does she do but botch it. It's enough to make a demon weep.' And I heard the old phoney give a sob. 'It's so difficult to find good agents these days – you have no idea.'

'Look,' I shouted, 'I don't want to hear your complaints – I have enough of my own.'

'Don't you feel for me at all?' he cried, and I could hear the great booby sobbing.

This is weird, I thought. He's actually weeping because Miss Black failed to kill me, and he's hurt because I won't sympathise with him. 'You're crazy, you know,' I shouted. 'You're out of your tree.'

'Oh, don't,' he wailed. 'You can be so cruel. And after all I've done for you!'

'You've done nothing for me, you bastard!' I shouted. 'You've done nothing but make life hell for me.'

'Have I really?' he said, suddenly cheerful. 'You're not saying that to cheer me up. Oh, you dear boy.'

'What are you on about now?' I bawled.

'Now you're being coy,' the fiend laughed, delightedly. 'No, you'll like Hell – and I'll be there to keep you company.'

'Have you said your piece?'

'Why yes, dear boy.'

'Well, get off the bloody line. I want to talk to Tia.'

He immediately changed his tune and sneered, 'Ah, your precious Tia. I could tell you something about your dear wife that would make your hair curl.'

'Yeah, yeah,' I said. 'We've sorted that out, Tia and I, and I'm satisfied that she didn't encourage your pathetic agent Tamati, but made it quite clear to him that whatever had been between them was over long ago.'

Sidewinder snorted. 'Whatever had been between them! They were lovers, damn it! They didn't fool around. They went the whole hog.' He laughed. 'And of course you believed her little fib! What an innocent you are! But that's part of your charm – not that it does anything to me.' He suddenly snarled. 'Enough of this badinage, delightful though it is. Listen to me – I have news for you.'

'What now?' I grumbled.

'Tia has seen the light.'

'Don't be a bloody fool!' I burst out laughing.

'You may well laugh,' he said, seriously. 'She's working for me now.'

'What are you talking about?' But he had unsettled me.

The fiend sighed. 'My time is almost up, and I'd lose face if I returned empty-handed. I have persuaded Tia to sell me *her* soul.' I gasped. 'It's in better shape than yours, so I think I've done pretty well.'

'Wait a minute,' I said. 'Let me get this straight. I think you're telling me a heap of shit. But that aside – are you saying she has actually agreed to sell you her soul?'

'That's correct,' he said, smugly.

'I don't understand.'

'Ah, but you will – it's beautifully simple.'

'What does she get out of it?' I almost groaned.

'Nothing.'

'Nothing!' I was astonished. 'What sort of a deal is that?'

'Hold your hat, dear boy, and I'll tell you.'

I gritted my teeth. 'I'm listening.'

'Well, you get to keep your soul, and, of course, I shall never trouble you again.'

I was so appalled I could say nothing.

'Beautiful, isn't it? This way, we shall all be happy.'

'You're lying,' I shouted. 'Tia would never enter into such a deal.'

'Ah,' he shouted, 'so you don't believe she loves you?'

'What's that got to do with it?'

'Don't be obtuse.'

'Look – you're confusing me. Let me think – '

'Take your time, dear boy.'

'Are you saying she has offered you her soul in place of mine?'

'Bingo! It's crazy, I know – but, yes, that's what I do mean.'

'You're lying – I don't believe you.'

'Why not ask the lady herself? Here she is.'

I heard him hand the phone to someone else, and I prepared myself to hear someone pretending to be Tia.

'Hello, darling.' There was no mistaking that voice. It was Tia. It was my darling Tia.

178

'Tia – tell me it's not true.'

'But, darling, it is true.' I groaned.

'You can bet your life on it,' gloated Sidewinder, in the background. 'The contract is signed and sealed.'

'But why did you do it – for God's sake, why?' Tears were running down my face.

'I did it for you, my darling. I hate to see you so unhappy. It tears at my heart.'

'But to sell your soul to the devil for me! How could you do it? I'm not worth it.'

I heard Sidewinder chuckling maliciously, 'That's one thing you got right! I'm enjoying this.' And I could hear him rubbing his palms together in glee. What a prize shit!

'Tia,' I pleaded, 'listen to me. I won't let you do it. You shouldn't have made such a terrible decision without discussing it with me.' And I babbled on while Sidewinder chortled in the background. I pleaded with him to tear the contract up. 'You can have my soul straight away.'

He laughed derisively. 'I don't want your wretched soul. I'm on to a good thing – the rarest of rare things, a pure soul!' He sniggered. 'And I have to say, dear boy – I owe it all to you.'

'You make me sick,' I shouted. 'You tricked her, you bastard.' I became incoherent with rage. 'How could you play your filthy tricks on an innocent girl?'

'You're the innocent one, dear boy,' he scoffed. 'She hops into Tamati's lustful arms, and you call her innocent. Wake up – you obviously don't know anything about women.'

I was exhausted. 'Why do you keep slandering her, when you know she has done nothing wrong?'

'Because I'm a demon, dear boy,' he laughed. 'You don't expect me to break my demonic oath, and praise the woman. I've never said a good thing about anyone in my life. It's more than my reputation is worth.'

'What reputation?' I mocked. 'From what you've told me in moments of self-pity you lost it long ago – if you've ever had it.'

179

'Now, that's unkind,' he grumbled. 'I take a ruined woman off your hands, and you abuse me. That's a fine thing to do to a friend.'

'Ruined!' I scoffed. 'That's a quaint word to describe anyone. It's positively Victorian.'

'Do you think so?' he said, eagerly. 'How kind you are. I'm crazy about the Victorians! There was more evil done then under the cloak of respectability than in any other period I know of. It was sheer hell.' He chortled fiendishly. 'They set a shining example to us all.' He clapped his hands for joy, then said, confidingly, 'You know, dear boy, I can't wait to get my hands on your wife's soul. This will undoubtedly be the high point in my life, the great goal towards which I've been working all along. Can you understand what it means to me? You're a generous man, I know, and I would be honoured if you were to say, "Well done, good and faithful servant."' I could hear the fiend blubbering. 'It would mean so much to me.'

'I would sooner kiss a toad,' I said, savagely.

'That was most unfriendly,' said the fiend, severely. 'But from the bottom of my snakehood, I forgive you.'

'You really hate women, don't you?'

'Well, now that you mention it,' he said, with a laugh. 'I suppose I do. That business in the Garden of Eden – it didn't reflect well at all on Eve. The trouble with women is that they aren't satisfied with being ignorant. Look at you – you're perfectly happy. No, the poor dears have to know it all. Where ignorance is bliss – and that sort of thing. It's so – what's the word? – unnecessary.'

'What are you talking about now?' I yelled. 'I don't want to hear any more.'

'I'm trying to do you a favour, dear boy,' he said, reproving me. 'If you knew as much about women as I do, you'd not miss Tia at all. You'd say good riddance.'

I could hear him chuckling to himself.

'You know, dear boy, you'll thank me one day for taking her

180

off your hands. Who knows – we might meet up one day, some-where, and talk about these times as among our happiest.'

'What utter bullshit!'

'When the ignorant are outwitted,' he said, sententiously, 'they resort to abuse.'

I don't know what Tia was doing while this idiotic conversation was going on. You could say I should have stopped it, and I suppose it's true, but what would that have served? I was hoping he would go too far and say something he'd regret – something I could use against him. There's a Higher Power I could appeal to, if he'd given me the slightest opportunity. Isn't there?

The fiend whistled. 'Are you there, dear boy? We really must bring this little chat, delightful as it is, to an end. Tia and I have plans to complete, and I must say she's been most cooperative. Not like you, old dear, snivelling and grizzling – ach! I can't understand why I bothered with you in the first place.'

'Go ahead – abuse me. I don't care anymore.'

'My dear boy,' he sneered. 'You bring tears to my eyes.'

'Be sarcastic, I don't care. Why did you bother with me at all,' I mumbled, 'if you have such a low opinion of me?'

'You know,' the fiend murmured, 'that's a good question. Let me see if I can answer it. You really want to know? It's purely academic now but it's of some interest, and it's simply told. Your grandfather, that meddling old fool, cursed your mother, accusing her of selling his pearls, and keeping the money for herself – quite unjustly, I have to say. Anyway, your mother died before the curse could take effect, and the curse, still very much alive, passed on to you.' He laughed, hollowly. 'And that's where yours truly came in.'

'Why me, and not my sister?'

'Your sister? What has she got to do with it?' he growled.

'Well, she's older than me. Shouldn't it have passed on to her?'

The fiend laughed. 'You are the one! What have you got against your sister?'

'Nothing – I'm very fond of her.'

'But you would rather she bear the curse, and not you?'

Was it possible? I wondered. I decided not to say anything.

'Anyway,' said the fiend, 'I can't answer that. I merely carry out orders, I don't make them.'

Yeah, I thought – like the concentration camp warders.

'What did you say?' he snarled.

'Nothing.'

'Take care,' he warned. Then he checked himself, and became quite affable, 'Tell me – were you a mother's boy?'

'Why do you want to know?'

'Just answer the question.'

'I suppose I was.'

'Well, there's your answer.' The fiend hummed happily to himself. 'I can't say I'm sorry it's over.' He paused and said, 'Are you there, old son? Is that you groaning?'

'Yes,' I shouted, 'I'm here – and I'm groaning. Pathetic, isn't it? You've broken my heart, you fiend.'

'Well,' he coughed, in embarrassment, 'it's nice of you to say so, but I'm only doing my job. I really must sign off now.'

'And I can't change your mind?' I was blubbering like a child.

'My dear chap – don't take it so much to heart. You'll find another woman. They are drawn irresistibly to grief. You'll have to fight them off.'

'Oh, shut up, you silly old trout. I want to speak to Tia. You can't turn me down.'

'It's the last time, mind.' He handed Tia the phone, murmuring, 'And they say that fiends are heartless!'

'Darling Tia.' My voice broke. 'I don't know what to do. It's absolutely terrible – I don't know what to do.'

'Oh, my darling,' she murmured, 'there's nothing you can do.'

'You got it!' rasped Sidewinder, in the background.

'I love you and always will, my darling,' she said, and I could hear her crying.

'But it's so terrible – to sell your soul to this piece of shit – this devil!'

'Careful,' growled the fiend.

'Why didn't you discuss it with me?'

'Don't answer that question,' snapped the fiend. 'He's already asked it.'

'You shut up,' I shouted at him. 'Darling, why didn't you talk it over with me?'

'Because I knew you'd try to talk me out of it.'

'But, darling, I've spoken to a urologist, who told me there's no reason why you can't have my baby. There are modern techniques that make it possible.'

'Oh, darling,' sobbed Tia, 'that's what I wanted most in the world. But now it's too late.'

'But is it too late?'

'Yes – it's too late.'

I groaned aloud. 'But what about Tieki? He'll be broken-hearted.'

'He's young enough for the hurt to heal quickly, and he'll have you to care for him.' I was now in tears. 'Promise me something,' she said.

'Anything, my love.'

'When you get over your grief – '

'I'll never get over it.'

'You will, my darling. And when you do, I want you to marry Nene. She's a lovely girl and perfect for you – and she'll be a good mother to my Tieki, and the twins and baby. Are you listening?'

'Yes.'

'Tell him,' gloated Sidewinder, 'go on – tell him of our plan.'

Tia was shocked. 'Do you really want me to tell him? It's so cruel.'

'You stupid girl – that's why I want you to tell him.'

'All right,' she said, 'but be it on your head.'

'Naturally,' the fiend burbled. 'Why should anyone else get the credit?'

'Darling – I'm to die in a plane crash, and it's then he'll take my soul.' And she burst into tears.

'No – not that,' I groaned, and then addressed my fiend. 'I appeal to you – take my soul, and let Tia go.'

'Is this a *rondeau*?' he said, coldly. 'No – it's out of the question, and we're ready to go. So wrap it up, you two. Time's up.'

After we'd hung up, I sat in my room, my head in my hands, too stunned to think. The cleaning girl drifted in and out, but I took no notice of her, and she was too considerate to break into my grief, with a thoughtless remark. But when she had finished, and I had thanked her, I noticed she had tears in her eyes.

Then, my head cleared, and I made up my mind to fly to Penrhyn and intercede with the fiend, and try to break the contract, and failing that to accompany Tia in a last-ditch attempt to foil the fiend. But, first, I had to speak to Tia.

I rang the exchange and asked the operator to put me through to Tia in Penrhyn, and I stressed the urgency. After fifteen minutes, Tia was talking to me. 'Hello, darling – it's really you, isn't it? I never expected to hear your voice again.'

'Tia,' I said, 'listen to me, darling. I have a plan – '

'You listen to me, buster,' rasped the fiend. 'You're wasting our time. The contract is unbreakable – so get off the phone.'

'Tia, darling,' I said, desperately, 'ignore the fiend, and listen to me. I'm flying back to Penrhyn, and I want you to wait for me. Don't board the plane until I've talked to you.'

'I don't know if I can do that,' said Tia, doubtfully. 'But I'll try.'

'What's going on, you two?' spluttered the fiend. 'This is highly irregular – '

'Oh, shut up,' I shouted. 'I'm flying back to Penrhyn, and you can't stop me. Tia, darling, do you know when the plane is arriving in Penrhyn?'

'At midday, I think.'

'OK – wait till I come.'

I had no time to spare, so I hurriedly dressed, grabbed my wallet, and ran to the office and left a message that I hoped to be back later in the day, and ran outside where I hoped to flag down a taxi. To my delight I found Muscles waiting in his ancient cab, its engine throbbing.

'This is a bit of luck,' I said, hopping in beside him. 'Airport, please. How did you know I'd be wanting a taxi?'

'I knew,' was all he said.

I knew the owner of a twin-engined Cessna, and at the airport I sought him out and begged him to fly me to Penrhyn. I told him it was a matter of life and death, which was true. He was very reluctant at first, because of the distance, but eventually he agreed when I offered him twice the normal fare, which I could ill afford.

Three hours later, we were circling above the airstrip at Penrhyn, and I could see a small crowd at the side of the runway where a small jet was waiting. The Cessna taxied to a standstill alongside the crowd, and no sooner was I on the tarmac than Tia was in my arms, kissing and hugging me.

'Oh, my darling – I'm so happy to see you. I never thought I'd see you again.'

I could see Tia's mother frowning at me, and I could almost hear her muttering, 'Why you make my daughter sad?' I knew that Tia hadn't told her of her pact with the fiend – how could she? So it wasn't surprising she looked bewildered. And the presence of the two aircraft, and my arriving on one, while Tia was waiting to fly out on the other, must have added to her confusion. The whole group stood silently looking on under the hot sun, like spectators at a game whose rules they didn't understand.

'Tia, what did you tell your mother?'

'I told her I needed to see a doctor in Rarotonga – and that's the truth. I haven't been well lately.'

'Where's Tieki? I don't see him about.'

'He went fishing with his Uncle Vaka. He didn't want to see me off. He was too upset.'

'Tia – I've got to talk to the fiend.'

She shook her head sadly. 'He won't talk to you. He says there's nothing to discuss, because the pact is binding, and can't be broken.'

'Then I must talk to the pilot,' but seeing the look of resignation in her eyes, I was beginning to feel that my mission was hopeless. 'If I can persuade him to refuse to take you, I might force the fiend to change his plans.'

But the pilot was no help at all. 'Say, what's going on? The lady asked me to fly her to Rarotonga, and I was happy to agree. Now you're sayin' not to take her. I'm a patient feller, but I don't take to being mucked about.' He was a genial, scraggy individual, with large grey muttonchops. He turned to Tia and said, 'See here, lady, I got a wife and kiddies with me, and we can't wait any longer. The heat is killin' us.'

I took Tia aside and said quietly, 'Listen to me. Aren't you morally bound to warn the pilot that his plane will crash if he takes you with him?'

'I could try, but it's unlikely he'll believe me.'

'Can I have a go?'

Tia was doubtful, but reluctantly agreed. Sidewinder – wherever he was – didn't intervene, and this gave me some hope that I might succeed.

What followed was one of the most embarrassing experiences of my life. When I told the pilot that his plane would crash if he took Tia, he was outraged. He thought I didn't trust either him or his jet, which was clearly the joy of his life. But when I went further and told him about Sidewinder's deal, he thought I was having him on, and became almost apoplectic, and I had to backtrack hurriedly, telling him it was only a joke.

'Some joke,' he retorted angrily. 'You must be some kind of nut.' He shook his head and said, 'It's up to the lady. If she wants to come with me, I'll be happy to take her.'

My head was spinning, and while Tia didn't say 'I told you so', her expression did.

I tried another tack. 'Can't we fly on the Cessna?'

'No, darling,' she said, shaking her head, sadly. 'It's in the contract. It must be the jet.'

'OK, then – I'm coming with you.'

'But you'll die, too, my darling. Please, don't come. Stay alive for Tieki's sake, if not for mine.'

'I've made up my mind – I'm coming with you.'

The look on the American's face was comical when I asked him if I could hitch a ride with him. 'First, you insult me and my plane, and then you ask for a ride.' He shook his head, and gave a raucous laugh. 'If that don't beat everything. Well, sir, when we get back to the States and try to describe what's happenin' here today, no one will believe me – but I guess I'll take you, if your friend over there,' indicating the Cessna pilot, 'will allow me.'

I spoke to the Cessna pilot, who was taken aback, but took it well enough. It was no skin off his nose, he grunted, provided he was paid the agreed fare.

And so it was time to go. The American who had been video-taping the crowd singing a farewell hymn rounded up his small family, then turned to me and pointed at his watch.

As we were saying goodbye, Tia's mother looked me in the eye and said, 'Why you taking my daughter away from me? My heart it tells me she won't come back.' And she turned away, and wept. And when we rose and circled the airstrip and flew south, I took away the memory of that devoted family group gathered together before the tall craggy figure of Uncle Hiro, who was leading them in prayer.

'Darling,' I said, holding her so tightly against me I almost crushed her, 'I'm holding on to you, and I'll never let you go. If the plane crashes, we'll both die, and not even Sidewinder can come between us. But, you know, I don't believe it will crash. There's been no sign of him. Perhaps he's had a change of heart.'

Tia sighed, and said, 'If only you were right, but I doubt it.' She paused and said, 'He said something really shocking to me today, just after you rang.'

'What did he say?'

'He said . . . ' Tia couldn't go on.

'Tell me,' I said, gently.

'He said, "I go to prepare a place for you," and he laughed.'

'But that's blasphemy.'

'Yes – it's blasphemy.' Tia shuddered. 'No, my darling – he hasn't had a change of heart. He hasn't got a heart.'

As if this was the signal the fiend was waiting for, the jet engine coughed, spluttered, died down, roared into life again, then failed altogether, and the aircraft began its downward plunge, causing the children who were playing in the aisle to tumble and crash screaming against the cockpit partition.

Their mother cried out, 'Oh, my God! Oh, my God!' and without thinking unbuckled herself to go to their rescue, just as the plane's nose dipped further, and she, too, lost her balance. I caught a glimpse of her husband's white horrified face, as her body crashed through the cockpit door, and slammed into him.

I remember little of what happened during the last few moments before the crash, except that throughout all the confusion and panic Tia thought only of me. 'Don't be afraid, my darling. Don't be afraid . . .'

'Nothing will ever tear us apart,' I vowed. But my heart was breaking.

After that, my mind went blank. I remember nothing more until I came to in the water, and was being helped aboard a fishing boat. At first I was confused and didn't know where I was, and how I got there. My head was badly gashed and bleeding, and I knew my right arm was broken, because I couldn't use it.

Then my memory flooded back, and I looked around for Tia. The pilot and his family, I noticed, were safe on board. The two children, white with shock, and bedraggled, clung to what remained of their mother's dress, and were sniffling miserably. But I couldn't see Tia anywhere.

'My wife's missing,' I shouted at our rescuers, small unkempt tough-looking men – Koreans, as I discovered later. 'For God's sake don't stand there. Look for her.' I must have run all over the ship, looking over the side, and scanning the sea in every direction, but there was no sign of Tia.

'Help me look for her,' I sobbed. 'We've got to find her.' But the fishermen stared blankly at me, and didn't move a muscle.

'They don't understand,' muttered the pilot, who had an ugly bruise on his forehead. 'They don't speak English.' He rubbed his eyes abstractedly, as if unable to take in what had happened.

'She's gone,' he muttered. 'I'm afraid she's gone . . . '

And as I stood there, stunned and confused, I heard his wife weeping.

A film of oil, a burst suitcase, torn clothing, some sheets of paper, pieces of joinery, and other debris floated on the calm water.

A frigate bird came from nowhere, swooped down to inspect the wreckage, screamed, and wheeled over the ship, and flew away.

But of my darling Tia there was not a sign. She must have died instantly when the aircraft struck the sea. Her body was never found.

Earlier titles in this trilogy:

THE FRIGATE BIRD

Alistair Campbell's first novel is set partly in the Cook Islands, partly in a New Zealand psychiatric hospital and partly within the confines of the narrator's mind. It is about a search – for love, sanity and the innocence of childhood – that continues through-out the whole trilogy. Along the way, we are introduced to some of the most bizarre and colourful characters to have appeared in Pacific fiction: Big Mouth, the Minotaur, Mr Soo and the demonic Sidewinder.

SIDEWINDER

In the second book in the trilogy, the narrator is now back in the Cook Islands and married to Tia, the woman he loves. Still endur-ing Sidewinder's persistent taunts and extravagant proposals, he becomes increasingly alarmed by the odd behaviour of two colourful imps called Belial and Beelzebub. His tantalising peace on the Pacific island paradise is imperilled as the story builds to an unexpected climax.

Alternating between the comic and the sinister, fantasy and mad-ness, Polynesian spirituality and European angst, The Frigate Bird and Sidewinder are among the most powerful works to have emerged from the Pacific area. Both were regional finalists for the Commonwealth Writers Prize.

Published by Reed in the Pacific Writers Series